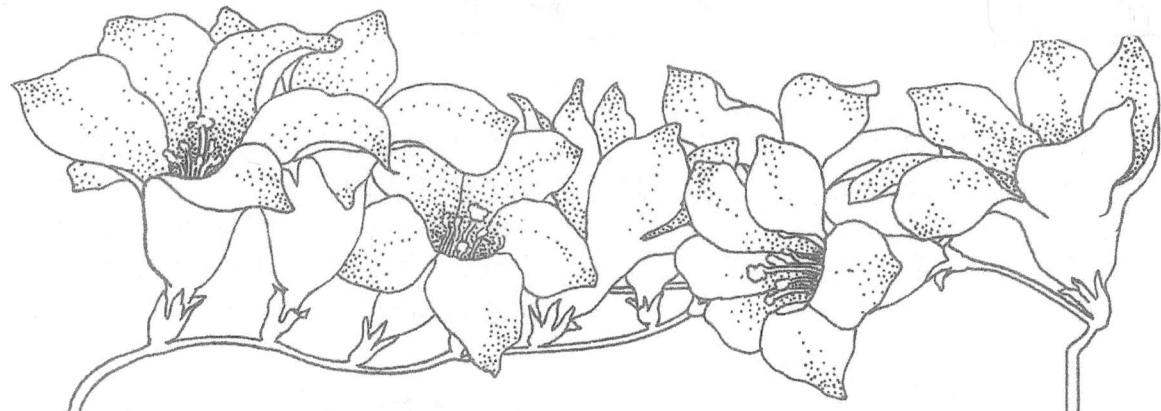

Greenwoman

A Literary Garden of . . .

Fiction ✽ Nonfiction ✽ Poetry ✽ Commentary

Biography ✽ Art ✽ Comics

Volume 4 - Garden Goddesses

Editor-In-Chief: Sandra Knauf
Deputy Editor: Zora Knauf
Copy Editor and Advisor: Cheri Colburn

Chief Designer: Sandra Knauf
Web Designer/Tech. Support: Paul Spielman
Cover Art by Paul Spielman

Advertising contact: Sandra Knauf
(719) 473-9237
sandra@greenwomanmagazine.com

Attn. retailers: For more information about selling this marvelous magazine in your store call 719-473-9237 or write sandra@greenwomanmagazine.com

Copyright 2012-2014 by Greenwoman Publications, LLC. All rights reserved. Reproduction in whole or in part without permission is prohibited.

Send comments, questions, concerns, and brilliant submissions of art and writing to:
Greenwoman Magazine, PO Box 6587, Colorado Springs, CO 80934-6587

ISBN-10: 0989705676
ISBN-13: 978-0-9897056-7-7

www.greenwomanmagazine.com
www.florasforum.com
www.zeraandthegreenman.com
www.greenwomanpublishing.com
www.gardenshorts.com

Contents

In Every Issue

Editor's Letter 3
Contributors 4
Top Dressing 72

Creative Nonfiction

A Generous Season 18
Diary of a Garden Goddess 44

Fiction

Lady in Waiting 10

Poetry

En Route 23
Chamomile Tea. 23
Perfect Eggs 20
Grow 34
Winter Garden 60

Art

Amaryllis in a Flask 16
Bees in the Barn 23
Spring Break 20
Tulips 33
Take to the Hills (cover) 36
"That which we have so greatly feared" . . 39
A Garden Daydream 45
Flight of the Yucca Moths 52
Yucca Mama and Yucca Moth
Make Contact 53
Naked Ladies 62
Red Rock Canyon in January 61
Conifers 66

Special Features

Amy's Other Art:
An Interview with Amy Stewart 24
Fire on The Mountain (a chapter excerpt
from *Take to the Hills*) 36

Essays & Columns

Slow Ride: The Seed, the Radicle, and
the Revolution 7
Hungry Chicken Homestead:
Poultry Season 8
Creature Feature: A Tale of Two Birds 21
Sex in the Garden:
An Underground Affair 63
Leafing Through (Reviews) 67

Comics & Etc.

Rockstars of Biology 29
Radish Gets Around 31
Food Don't Waste It 43

Cover art by Paul Spielman.

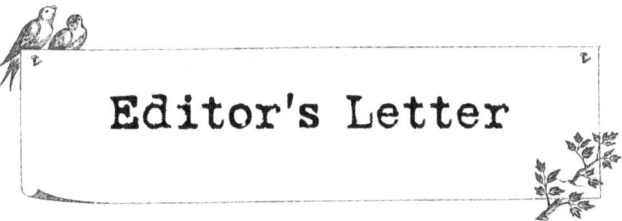

Editor's Letter

What a year! It's been an especially ambitious and dramatic one at my house. On the breaking-new-ground list I tried something new at the community garden. Inspired by *The 50 Mile Bouquet*, I wanted to see how many organically-grown flowers I could grow in our challenging climate in a few square feet (about 100). I ordered dahlia starts, bought sunflower and zinnia seeds, and, after months of nurturing, the experiment came to fruition. Several fresh bouquets a week graced our home and office from mid-July through September. I gave many more to friends, business assoicates (often one and the same), and we supplied 18 arrangements for our locally-grown food celebration.

The biggest new project, though, was, under my daughter/Deputy Editor Zora's encouragement, deciding to publish my young adult novel, *Zera and the Green Man*. This book—a sci-fi fantasy mix of ancient dieties and a chosen teenager battling with an unscrupulous biotech multi-national corporation—had been over a decade in the making. Frankly, with the magazine work, I was ready to shelve the novel for good. It had been in limbo for two years when Zora read it and said, "Mom, you have to publish this. I will *help* you." Five months of reading the novel out loud, rewriting, getting a cover design (thank you, Paul Spielman), and working on a hundred other details followed.

I am so lucky to have such a daughter who says, "Just do it, Mom." This is especially notable since Zora has had plenty going on with her own ambitions. She'll conquer four years of college in three (thanks to the International Baccalaureate program at Palmer High School) so these last months she's been applying to grad schools while also applying for scholarships for a Study Abroad program in Cork, Ireland (University College) for her last semester at CU Boulder. Her sister Lily is following in her footsteps, graduating in May from high school (then I shall truly be an empty nester!) and *she's* thinking of adventuring west to school in California—or New York. It's not easy seeing these strong, adventurous daughters grow up. It's not easy for their dad either, but we are both bursting with happiness for them.

We did all this while enduring a Colorado wildfire that came (literally) into our city, the Aurora tragedy, another nasty election season, and an ongoing battle with those who would gladly despoil El Paso County for a few fracking dollars (nevermind the potential we have here for wind and solar power). At times it was such a relief to escape to work on *Greenwoman*! I think you'll be pleased with the result. This issue delves into different eras: the 1920s (Rebekah Shardy's amazing fictional diary of one woman's transformation), the 1940s (a chapter from one of Ozark chronicler Marguerite Lyon's memoirs), and a turn-of-this-century "diary" (from *moi!*) about working as gardener-for-hire when my girls were little. I think you'll find the issue a sweet escape, and I hope, an inspiration.

Sandra

Sandra Knauf, Editor and Publisher

Mom/Editor-Daughter/ Deputy Editor clowning around at the photo booth. Manitou Springs Arcade, November 23, 2012

Contributors

Full-time artist **Theresa Bayer** creates whimsical acrylic paintings, ink drawings, and caricatures, in Austin, Texas. See her work at www.tbarts.com/

Jill Bates grew up on Crooked Lake in Kalamazoo, Michigan, and now lives with her husband as a year round resident of Cape Cod. She loves to paint the natural world and writes, "I am most interested in painting the many moods and color changes of different bodies of water . . . I am always trying to capture an elusive transparency that allows you to see the surface and under the water at the same time." www.jillbatespastels.com/

Lucy Bell is a retired teacher and writing consultant. She is a certified Native Plant Master and leads interpretive nature walks at Colorado's Cheyenne Mountain State Park and Red Rock Canyon. She founded "Friends of Emerson," a reading and discussion group.

Born in Rochester, NY, **Laura Chilson** graduated with her BFA from SUNY Purchase School of Art+Design in 2008. She currently resides in Ithaca, NY. She specializes in pencil portraits and oil paintings and can be reached through her website, www.LauraChilson.com.

Becky Elder owns Blue Planet Earthscapes, an award-winning organic gardening company, and is a well-known activist in her local community. Certified in permaculture design, Becky co-founded and is co-Director of Pikes Peak Permaculture. Her Manitou Springs, Colorado, gardens are National Wildlife Federation's certified wildlife habitat. Her first book, *Raven in the Garden, a Front Range Gardener's Journal* was published in 2007.

Jane Knechtel has worked as a psychotherapist and serves on the Board of Directors of *In Other Words* Feminist Community Center in Portland, Oregon, one of nine remaining feminist bookstores left in the country (there were over 200 in 1980). Her work has appeared or is forthcoming in *The Sunday Oregonian*, *The Tar Wolf Review*, *Reed: A Journal of Poetry & Prose*, *Fire* (U.K.), *Woman Made Gallery*, *The Tusculum Review*, and others. Her many honors and awards include the 2006 Parnell Prize in Poetry and the 2008 Donn Goodwin Poetry Prize.

Elisabeth Kinsey teaches writing online, lives in Denver, pines away for Half Moon Bay, and publishes in *The Denver Post* and various journals. Her hands are imminently dirty. She may or may not be related to the late Dr. Alfred Kinsey.

Contributors

Amanda Laughtland is the author of *Postcards to Box 464* (Bootstrap Productions) and the editor/publisher of Teeny Tiny Press. She teaches English at Edmonds Community College, just north of Seattle.

Dan Murphy is a seasoned zine writer (*The Juniper*, *Elephant Mess*) and proponent of the slow life. His long-time passions include bike riding, skateboarding, punk rock, and gardening. His new interests include botany, ecology, wildflowers, and lichens. Dan has a B.S. in horticulture and an M.S. in biology (his thesis was on green roof technology research). He works at the Idaho Botanical Garden in Native Plant Horticulture. Learn more about Dan at www.juniperbug. blogspot.com

Jennifer Newcomb Marine is an author and a blogging and marketing coach. She's the new Marketing and Community Manager of *Daily Paintworks*.

Robin Peterson's artwork may be seen at www.fernwoodstudio.com or www.dailypaintworks. com/Artists/robin-peterson-1798. A lifelong study of animals and the natural world informs and inspires her work as an illustrator and painter.

Zoe Tilley Poster describes herself as "an artist, gardener, and wanderer of the woods" and describes her blog, (www.pearledearth.blogspot.com) as a place to "record those notions which take a brief roost in my brain before fluttering out the exit ear and away on the wind." You can find her art at www.etsy.com/shop/zoetilleyposter

Rancher/writer **Tom Preble** lives in his self-built, earth-bermed, and energy-efficient home and ranch on the Palmer Divide east of Colorado Springs. Something of a Renaissance man, Tom has wide ranging interests from astronomy to welding to philosophy. Trained as a computer electronics engineer and now semi-retired, Tom drives a school bus over the backroads of the Colorado prairie and observes and writes about his little friends on the bus. www.tompreble. com/

DB Rudin is an environmental education consultant, elementary school teacher, and the Education Coordinator at Venetucci Farm, an 190-acre historic farm in Colorado Springs, Colorado. He offers programs through Colorado Critter Encounters, which includes hands-on programs for kids on nature and conservation, and a class for those who tend the soil, The Good, the Bad and the Beautiful: Bugs 101 for Gardeners. www.cocritterencounters.com

Contributors

Rebekah Shardy, author of *98 Things A Woman Should Do in Her Lifetime*, was nominated for Excellence in Arts for Poetry by the Pikes Peak Arts Council and was awarded first place for short fiction by Authorfest of the Rockies. In 2007, she received the "Community Builder" award from the Colorado Springs Arts, Business and Education (ABE) Consortium for creating and presenting free creative writing workshops (The Mighty Muse Writing Project for Women) to 300 survivors of domestic violence, addiction, and incarceration.

Bonnie Simon writes about locally-owned businesses, the power of community, and the American dream in Colorado Springs, Colorado. Her business, Hungry Chicken Homestead, helps locally-owned businesses tell their stories and connect with consumers. Read more about Bonnie and the chickens at www.HungryChickenHomestead.com.

Paul Spielman says he is a long-time coffee-house sketcher, doodler, Arch-Top electric guitar player, and genuine Art-School graduate (who was lucky enough to study under Ron Lucas). But mostly he is a puzzled people-watcher. He makes his home in Colorado Springs, Colorado, with his wife Sri, who is an artist and retired florist.

Larry Stebbins is the founder and director of Pikes Peak Urban Gardens, a botanist, and a retired science teacher. He has over 40 years experience as a biodynamic and organic gardener.

Rhonda Van Pelt is a journalism veteran, most recently writing about art, theater, and nonprofits for the *Colorado Springs Independent*. Rhonda tries to do something creative every day, and she enjoys celebrating nature through her photography and quilts.
Visit her website at www.rhondashouseofcreativity.shutterfly.com/

Carolyn Williams-Noren's poems have appeared in *Greenwoman Magazine*, *Spoon River Poetry Review*, *Literary Mama*, and elsewhere. Her poem "Mistakes" received a 2009 Pushcart Prize nomination from *Seems*, and in 2010 E. Ethelbert Miller and Kristin Naca selected her work for a Loft Mentor Award. She lives and gardens in Minneapolis with her husband and two daughters.
.

Sylvia Woods lives in Oak Ridge, Tennessee, and teaches English. Sylvia's work has appeared in magazines and anthologies including *Southern Poetry III: Appalachia* and *Cornbread Nation V*. She has work forthcoming in *Southern Poetry IV: Tennessee*. She is a founding member of the Gap House Writers.

The Seed, the Radicle, and the Revolution

Many people are familiar with the "one straw revolution" proposed by (the late) Japanese rice farmer Masanobu Fukuoka, but what about the simple, revolutionary powerhouse that is the seed? Seeds have often been referred to metaphorically when discussing revolutions, new movements, new beginnings, social change, and spiritual awakenings. It only makes sense that the first thing to emerge from a seed during germination is the embryonic root known as the radicle (pronounced "radical"). It has been said that it only takes one individual to start a revolution. It only takes one seed to start a forest. The process may be slow, but the potential is there.

A tiny seed finds its way into a small crack in the sidewalk. The radicle emerges. Before you know it, a plant strong enough to push apart two concrete slabs has grown. A radical radicle pushes headlong through a pile of dirt and muck that has collected in a rain gutter on a rooftop. Up sprouts a renegade plant, adamant about making a human-made structure its home.

Devastation can come in the form of a seed; ruins can be made of structures that were ignorantly thought of as eternal. Radicals rise up as radicles force themselves downward, rooting in new lives, and readying themselves for battle. Yes, the seed is revolutionary.

Words are like seeds, and their influence can cause a social sea change as the message spreads. The *Juniper* zine is microscopic proof of that. The *Juniper* is my tiny eco-zine—a meager cut-n-paste publication printed on a copy machine and sent out around the world to interested folks—promoting the small, simple, slow life and encouraging the masses to grow it from seed and get here by bike. As letters have

> Words are like seeds, and their influence can cause a social sea change as the message spreads.

by
Dan Murphy

trickled in to the *Juniper*'s mailbox, this editor has noticed a thriving (albeit grassroots) social movement as readers have recounted their stories of gardening, biking, and going back to the land.

Rusty bikes have been retrieved from dusty storage areas, tuned up, and taken for a ride. Derelict areas of backyard lawn have been turned over, and gardens have sprouted up. The slow life is spreading just as fast as the seeds can germinate, and off we sprint toward ecotopia.

Spring is for sowing seeds and encouraging growth. Love is in the air, and heaven knows that the revolution needs much more of that. Cynicism can be brushed away for a while. Spring cleaning allows us to pull some of our skeletons out of their hiding spots and send them packing. It's okay to feel overwhelmed while we're at it.

Certainly a seed recognizes the pressure that lies on its tiny self to thrive, flourish, and produce. But there is potential in all of us; potential that will not be compromised: neither blacked-out by black hearts nor whited-out by whitewash.

The subversive seed and its radical roots will be our mascot. Let's make our gardens grow. Let's not rot in the soil, but instead sprout and rise up. Your neighborhood will be your seedbed. That's where the movement starts. ✿

Poultry Season

by Bonnie Simon

As fall begins and the daylight wanes, my chickens start molting and stop laying eggs. I haven't eaten an egg in weeks, but nature is seasonal. Earlier in the year, the peaches ripened and we ate, cooked, and canned as many as we could. Later it was frozen beans and pickled cucumbers, but what all this produce has in common is a season that begins and ends. So it is with eggs. The chickens lay a few in the winter, peak in the summer, and stop in the fall.

Two years ago, I brought these four birds home as two-week old chicks. When I told people I was getting chickens, we always had some variation of this conversation: "Are you getting them as pets or for eggs?"

"Oh, they are livestock," I would reply. "They'll provide eggs, and then I'll eat them when they get older."

The other person, especially if she had known me a long time, would smile indulgently and suggest that I was more likely to open a Chicken Retirement Home.

Sure enough, the laying hens became pets and I learned from farmers this isn't uncommon. A three year old hen of a breed known for eggs yields tough meat and a certain amount of sadness at slaughter. You've cared for her a long time and gotten to know her, maybe she even has a name. It's hard to let her go. If you want meat, it makes more sense to buy a batch of "meat bird" chicks. They've been bred to mature in six weeks and, if not slaughtered, die of heart attacks soon after. It's easier to maintain an emotional distance and you get the added advantage of meat that's good for more than stew.

The transition from livestock to pets began when I gave my chicks names. It happened naturally, as I watched them grow and I learned to tell them apart by the feather patterns on their heads. They became Redhead, Specklehead, Blonde Chicken, and, because her head was somewhere between red and blonde, Middle Chicken.

When they grew into their feathers and out of the brooder, I built them a coop, affectionately referred to as "Chicken Shantytown." Chicken Shantytown consists of a long cage made of hardware cloth with homemade doors at both ends. I've boxed in four feet with plywood and straw to protect them from the weather and provide some privacy for laying eggs.

Technically, this 30 square foot coop offers enough space for four hens, but every morning they squawk at the door, dragging their beaks along the wire, like prisoners with tin cups.

"Let us out of Chicken Jail!" I imagine they are saying. "We're innocent!"

They are. And so I do.

All day long, my little bird-friends roam around the backyard, doing what chickens were born to do. They run around and flap their wings. They eat all the kitchen scraps in what used to be the compost pile. They hold meetings under the deck. They make me laugh and remind me how to greet every day as an opportunity for something good.

And don't forget about the eggs.

During the summer, they gave me so many eggs, I started tipping service providers with them.

"Here's the check for the invoice, and these fresh eggs are for you," I'd say, starting yet another conversation about the novelty of keeping chickens in the city.

"What made you decide to get chickens?"

"I can't explain it," I always say. "It seemed like the right thing."

In this middle season of my life, I want the simplicity and quiet to hear God speak. I want to live like the chickens, expressing the best of my nature. I'd had enough of the rat race and its mirage of success. I wouldn't trade my homestead and the chickens for any of its offerings.

Every day, they remind me to be grateful for that freedom. ❈

Sadie & Ruby ♥ Greenwoman Magazine

Sadie: My mind's still reeling from the thought-provoking articles and stories I read last night.

Ruby: Mine too! *Greenwoman*'s a great mind trip.

Sadie: Can't wait for the next volume. . .

Ruby: Neither can I.

FREE download when you sign up!

Let's Stay in Touch!

Available through Amazon.com (if that's how you roll).

We can do just that if you sign up for our weekly newsletter at www.greenwomanmagazine.com.

Read Online (the greenest option) for only $2.95 an issue!

In return, we'll send you garden writing fabulousness, special offers on our books, and more!

Lady in Waiting:
A Journal of Curious Transmutation

by
Rebekah Shardy

Illustration by Theresa Bayer

**S**eptember 3, 1926

As I washed this morning, I was startled by the abhorrent sight of an errant hair just below the diamond of my pert chin. As Colette says, "It's mighty difficult to retain the characteristics of one's sex after a certain age." Damned Saturn! I mused aloud to my pet Pomeranian while steadying the tweezers. Saturn is, of course, the god of time who eats his own children—but not until they are disagreeably disfigured, it would seem, and pretty maidens are made into men.

Despite my ire, this—thing!—would not pull free. On closer inspection, I saw it was not a familiar hair, black and wiry as the nether region of the Devil's groin, but a spongy tendril!

I won't listen to Franz go on anymore about my diet. I've quit his maniacal vegetarianism if sprouting vines is what comes of it! Let him think me fat! After coming home he rarely leaves the study. The post delivered another anatomy book—filled, I discovered, with the comely calves and unspeakables of the *corpus femina*. Really.

October 26, 1926

All I desire to eat are napoleons. I seem to take erotic pleasure in food, plundering freely that which lies passively on my plate, quite incapable of ravaging me.

The new neighbor, in scandalous red stockings and pince-nez glasses, brought me a bit of superstition wrapped in a lace hanky: Devil's Bit Root tea. She quotes the fable that says its stubby root was bit by the Devil in a fit of jealousy for its healing power to help both the bloody womb and dry.

"Avoid envy," she warns, wagging a crooked finger. "It's the bane of older women, causing bitterness and disturbance of the gall-bladder."

Am I old? It is true I am nearly 50, but I pray I won't become a witch like that ruddy crone. Perhaps it's too late. At the most unexpected moments, and in particular when Franz goes into a petulant tirade, I feel flames of heat blossoming inside, as if I were already tied to the heretic's stake.

> "... I feel flames of heat blossoming inside, as if I were already tied to the heretic's stake."

November 15, 1926

Fighting with Franz. It chills me through and through when he calls me "Mother." Have I begun to wear my hair in black crepe ribbon? No, but I must now remove an entire flowerbed of tendrils from my chin each morning, rising early so no one will perceive anything amiss. I am loath to discard them, studying them with the tender looks reserved for one's infants. Placed a few in a water glass in my gardening shed.

That meddling neighbor must have heard our marital acrimony. She appeared at the shed door with another hanky, this one embroidered with pansies and containing what she calls "Adam-and-Eve Root. Break off the part that looks like a man's printle and protect it; give the female leafed-half to the Mister for safekeeping and your bond will remain sure." She actually winked at me.

I placed the printle in my locket and the Eve-piece in Franz's neglected humidor.

December 22, 1926

It is the holiday and I am quite weary of the idea. Instead of inviting the family to dinner and going to church, as proper, I have informed everyone that I am sick with pleurisy. I lie abed listening to the howling wind outside, entertaining myself with imaginary conversations and deliberate acts of rebellion that I would never execute by light of day.

The crone came to see me. I fully expected her to bring a godforsaken horseradish root to make a chest poultice, but she looked at me knowingly and pulled out a flask of blackberry brandy, instead. "Loose lips often ease tight lungs," she whispered, and commenced to smooth the sheets comfortingly while waiting for me to imbibe.

For two hours, while I twisted my bedclothes in my hands, fretting and sputtering with anger about this and that, she patted my snoring Pomeranian, quietly nodding or adding, "My word, yes . . ." now and then. My own dear mother is dead, but she could not have been as solicitous and kind as this wise woman of my boudoir.

When no more could be spilled, from either lips or bottle, she made ready to leave. "You'll be just fine, but no one will hear it from me," she said, ensuring my confidence. Instead of giving me something for my faux-pleurisy, she brought out the most disgusting thing: a cross, it appears, between a man's member and a sea urchin.

"Solomon's Seal Root," she explained. "Boil it twice and use it to remove those nasty spots that besmirch a lady's hands and face as she grows wise." Meaning old, of course. Thankfully, she has become more discreet in her choice of words.

"I am resolved: I will make a tea from the strange little plants hidden like forbidden liqueurs in the shed."

January 4, 1927

I'm quite sad today for dissimilar reasons. I became acutely aware in bath this morning that my bosom, still as soft as a seraphim's cheek, is as fallen as Lucifer's hope of heaven.

Secondly, the Vicar stopped by and reported that my crone, Mrs. Wycliffe-Benson, is in hospital. I'd become quite attached to her impulsive visits. Franz does not like company, so I am never free to invite her for tea and must make do with her odd little notes tied to the branches of the hazel tree or left in a geranium pot at the door.
I decided to make her a gift to cheer her—elecampane candies from crushed elfwort sweetened with honey. Pliny, Elder of Rome, claimed that the root "expels sorrow and causes mirth."

I was preparing the candy in the shed when I suddenly noticed the glass containing my chin "hairs"—if that is what they are. I dropped the chopping knife in alarm, narrowly missing my foot, as I saw they are boldly sprouting as robustly as potatoes!

Their color is the palest green, like a certain shadow I sometimes see crossing the moon's face, or the tint in early pear. Their little bodies are plump and square, certain to take root. I planted them in fine terra cotta pots from Italy, a gift from a dear friend from girlhood, and found myself singing Puccini's aria, 'Sempre Libre''

Franz nearly shattered the study's pane-glass, so hard did he slam it shut against my music.

January 29, 1927

Am I growing stout and querulous? It is a wonder my gall-bladder does not burst, I have become so bitter with recollection of the occupations I cherished before life with Franz: painting in Northern Italy with Cherisse, teaching French at the finishing school, studying opera with Mr. Carrolton who said he'd rather sacrifice his selfish happiness than spoil my young voice with the mundane compromises of wedded life.

I hear Mrs. Wycliffe-Benson has grown worse and hardly stirs from her hospital bed. If it were me she would have brought me some obscure elixir by now meant to awaken a torpidly disagreeable Sleeping Beauty.
I am resolved: I will make a tea from the strange little plants hidden like forbidden liqueurs in the shed. They have pushed out tiny leaves, like perfect gloves, sparkling emerald. Tears spring to my eyes at even the thought of crushing them.

My nether-region floods have stopped entirely. I wonder if the blood has instead moved to my head, which feels tight and pained. Occasionally, my heart beats as erratically as if a mouse were trapped inside its red lacquered box, desperate for release.

I peek into my locket and see that the printle in which I placed so much expectation is as desiccated as a neglected hangnail. I think Franz mistook the Eve-root for a shred of tobacco. The humidor is empty, and his study reeks of stale smoke. He would puff my heart away if it brought him a moment's distraction.

February 10, 1927

Amazing story. The tea I made for Mrs. Wyatt-Benson from my mysterious cuttings resulted in her dramatic recovery! Since the Sabbath I visited the dear, ladling my golden broth into her tidy cat-mouth, she has become progressively vital and alert. I visit her daily at her son's home, the Andrew Benson, Esq., with my endless supply of tea.

I am myself much better, although my undressed flesh has taken on a waxy sheen and oddly porous texture.

At night, my sleep is plagued with dreams about enormous caves and tender-eyed trolls. The light often makes my eyes sore, so I lie down at midday, somnolent as a turnip in its kitchen basket.

Franz says I need to take a holiday, but I feel too ponderous to move about as travel requires. I also fear the heat of the Mediterranean climate, yearning to lie down in a place not only dark, but also damp and cool.

March 21, 1927

Scandalous. Aroused by Spring, I stood barefoot and clad only in my nightgown in the cold, pungent dirt of the disheveled garden like a bold weed. Impelled by some imp of outlandish instinct, I spied a wild leek and fought with the damp earth for its purchase, biting into its raw white root. God, it stunk like secret sex and bit me back on my tongue with its maliciously strong meat.

The Swedes call it Ramsom Root—so named because it grows under the constellation of Aries the Ram. Even as I stood there, reveling in my impetuosity, Franz fetched the doctor. I would say nothing to say to either of them with all their rude prying and prodding.

"You don't want to live on the surface of things, anymore, do you dear?"

Franz finally sent for Mrs. Wycliffe-Benson, completely well and at home once more. She looked me over twice (once closely in the eyes) and announced: "You don't want to live on the surface of things, anymore, do you, dear? Your heart is yearning for the return."

Return of what?

"To your root! To the end and beginning, to Mystery and her fecundity of soul. Transformation! The change of life, dear. If you're not too afraid, that is."

"I didn't think I had a choice," I said weakly.

"Oh, there are choices, alright," she said, pressing a candied ginger candy into my hand as she rose to leave. "Only you can choose to go deep. Only you can want to drink the hidden waters."

"And what of you?" It was an impertinent question, but she only laughed.

"Do you think I always looked like this? I have had my transformation, too, child. Once, I was slender as a new cherry tree and tears had not diluted the skies of my eyes. I avoided serious talk and would never plant a flower for fear of dirtying a finger. And I would have never walked up to your door because the step was cracked and your curtains look dingy. My change of life was into one who knows life with her hands and heart, a Mage of bitter-tasting medicine and words, her face rough and gnarly as a healing root."

That very night I dreamt of an underground river. I was in an emerald boat with Cherisse who rowed us along the dark stream, redolent of hyacinth, as she sang a French lullaby. I was awakened by the sound of my own laughter and did not recognize it at first . . . I had forgotten its sound.

May 2, 1927

I no longer sleep. I wander about at night when it is pleasurably cool, and sleep during the day with the blinds shut tight against the sun. The window in the garden shed is pressed from the inside by a wild thicket of green. I could not even push open the door for the bushy tree spreading uncouthly within. I am terrified to realize that it is the cuttings from my own body that is fighting to leave the shuttered shed and spread its fertility through the lanes and thickets, tangled and green. What unnamable, bewildering thing have I become?

My dreams are of jungles, scarlet hibiscus and screaming parrots. I toss and turn, and Franz says he must sometime go out to avoid the sound of my cries—they disturb his sensibilities. He leaves laudanum by the bedroom door but I do not touch it. I fear I am already half-mad with these strange visions and desires for green on green on green . . .

June 13, 1927

Mrs. Hyatt-Benson has just left. She says she can bear it no longer to see me suffer. She says I have made my choice, and she will help me to return to my source. Am I truly ready to leave Franz, and my comfortable life with him, for what I do not yet know?

I tell her I am already a stranger to him, and the life I once led is now repellent. I have only one desire, and it is too strange to speak.

She begs me to tell it, and I feel I can trust this odd woman above all others. I lead her to the bedroom window and point down to the garden.

"There," I say. "That is what I want."

She is as solemn as the Vicar when she leaves, but I believe she understands me. She says she will return in September, under the Dark Moon. She says she will help me make the final transformation.

I feel ripe. And for once, in a very long time—excited.

September 29, 1927

Like that brazen tenant of Eden, I lured Franz into the garden last night and tried to seduce him. The idea of pushing up against his heavy darkness from the dewy dirt stirred an avid feeling in me.

He only sighed and asked if I still had any of that red cabbage cooked in vinegar. Between my weedy chin and my tight, rounded flesh, he thinks, of course, of his beloved vegetables.

Tonight, the crone came and did not even speak about our pact. She knows my heart and its secrets the way she understands the hidden tonics of roots. She brought a silver shovel, slender and pretty in its way. I am excited to join her and must leave this writing for now. Until the next adventure—

EPILOGUE

They took turns digging a deep, long slit in the black earth while crickets chanted and a night bird awakened. The crone took both of her hands and pulled her toward her as if they were going to dance. Instead, she was led down into the hole, the old womb of earth, where she had longed to stretch out for months. Like a mother, the crone tucked her into that bed, pulling down the earth and patting it over her.

She could hear the old woman grunt from the effort. Oh, how wonderful the pressure of rich loam must have felt —like a velvet coverlet embracing her with the promise of wonderful dreams!

Just before the final shovel of dirt closed the air above her, she whispered, "Wait. Will you pull me up when I am ready?"

"Ready?"

"When it is the right moon and season to make some medicine of me, to give some poor woman wrapped in your handkerchief like a baby in swaddling." She had loved those dirt-smudged gifts.

"You didn't know? My dear, the only healing you are meant to bring is for you! You are becoming the root that can heal your own heart. You will blossom again."

And then the sowing was done. She heard the crone's feet above her and shivered. So cold! And then, slowly and at last, the blissful warmth of home!

Something deep inside her womb pushed out and down—a twisting but painless birth of sorts. She put out a tap-root. Spiraling down, deep and deeper into the earth, it was seeking, spreading and yearning toward the underground rivers.

Village authorities persistently questioned Franz after his wife vanished. He was released from custody but never from the suspicions of the town people so he left to go abroad.

While his wife germinated, seasons came and left behind their gifts. A doe and her fawn slept in summer in the hollow of grass where she lay; one spring, a flock of goldfinches busied themselves about the garden as they gleaned each rose hip from the neglected roses. A fox sniffed close by with tears in his eyes. A full moon left her calling card of dew each month as she slept deep and well below.

Eventually, Melissa Trudell and her new husband moved in. The young woman loved to spend her evenings walking the garden, even in the chill of fall when a little owl sat in the Japanese willow murmuring forlornly. It's like Something draws me there, she told her curious spouse.

The first pregnancy was complicated and she was forbidden to leave the house, and then was confined to her bed. Still, on waking and before sleeping, she would steal to her window where she could gaze on the lovely garden with longing.

It was during these tedious hours in bed that she found the diary. Where can she be? My friend that I have never met who lives in the garden I love?

One night, while her spouse snored gently beside her, she slipped from bed, a full moon herself, enormous in her white nightgown, floating through the dark.

She wandered the cricket-sung garden, feeling the velvet and satin of leaves around her until her eyes grew accustomed to the shadows. How could she have missed it? A stand of shocking pink flowers, more strongly scented than phlox, yet delicately wistful as lilac.

Never before had she noticed them.

She kneeled to embrace the blooms and felt the kick of the unborn child.

Finding his wife out of bed and prone in the garden, her husband called for the doctor. After Melissa gave birth to a vigorously healthy girl – Flora Blossom Trudell – beside the happy flowers, she whispered something just out of range of hearing.

The doctor bent close to her lips to catch her words of exhaustion.

"Yes? Are you alright, Mrs. Trudell?"

It didn't make sense to him: words of a foreign language. Italian, he later discovered.

The words of an opera that haunts carefully cultivated gardens and women:

Sempre Libre. Always free. ❀

From *Handbook of Nature Study*, 1947.

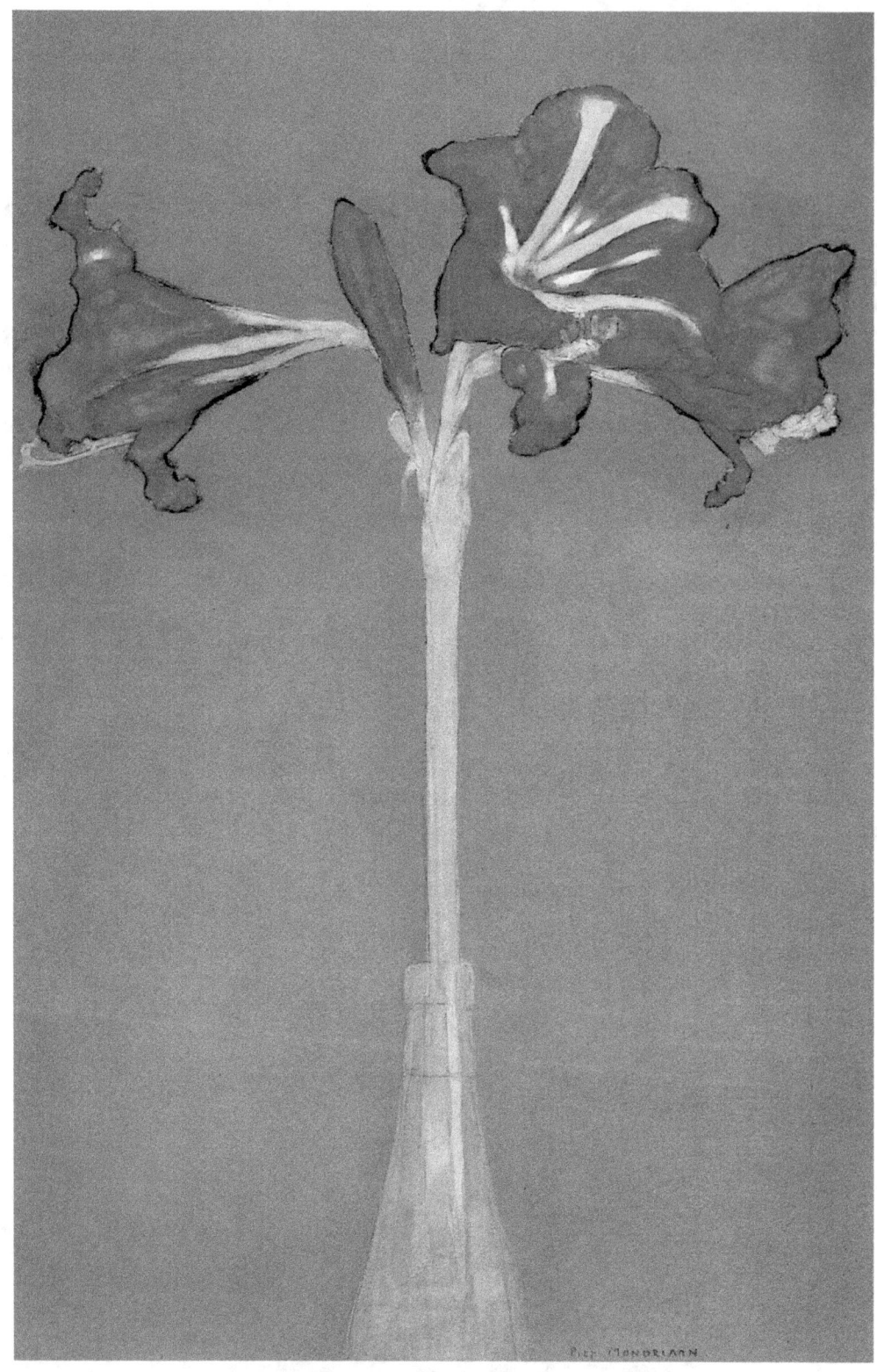

Piet Mondrian (1872-1944)
Amaryllis in a Flask in Front of a Blue Background.
c. 1909

THE NEXT TIME SOMEONE TELLS YOU GENETICALLY ENGINEERED CROPS, ALSO KNOWN AS GMOs, ARE NEEDED TO FEED THE WORLD, ASK THEM TO FURNISH EVEN A SINGLE REPUTABLE STUDY THAT SHOWS GMOs HAVE REDUCED WORLD HUNGER SINCE THEY WERE INTRODUCED IN 1996.

 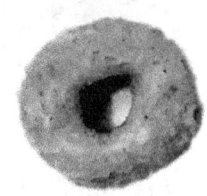 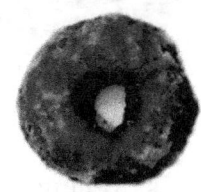

Today's GMOs are mainly used for ethanol fuel, animal feed, & processed junk foods. Those things don't feed the world.

JOIN US TO LEARN ABOUT THE MYTHS & TRUTHS OF GMOs AND HELP US CHANGE THE FOOD SYSTEM.

GMO
FREE
USA

www.gmofreeusa.org
www.facebook.com/gmofreeusa

A Generous Season
by
Tom Preble

A gentle rain is falling. It's evening now and all is quiet—too quiet! With every passing moment, the garden, the malignant garden is growing. We've warned friends to watch out, that the squash vines may be growing faster than they can run! Savvy friends visiting our ranch know about our squash problem and lock their cars, lest their back seats somehow mysteriously become filled with zucchini, neatly stacked like cord wood.

My sweetheart has far too green a thumb, way too much of a good thing. She tries to blame our composted chicken crap from our hens for bursting garden beds. I tell her she's being ridiculous. "If chicken crap could cause such growth, why we'd have redwood trees at work!"

And yet her pansies and cosmos have hurdled log-end edging and are marching out into the gravel drive. I've warned her that I'm close to classifying these as noxious weeds and considering getting after them with a jug of herbicide and the weed eater! But her pleas for mercy melt my resolve . . . Meanwhile johnny jump-ups huddle and plot from under the front deck.

Our garden is planted right up to our bedroom windows. Just outside, huge waving zucchini leaves and six foot sunflower stalks resemble the flags and standards of a besieging Roman army. Snap dragons crowd the bottom edge of the living room picture window, peeping in at us. Petunias and marigolds riot in barrels on the front deck.

"I just don't know what to say," my sweetheart offers. "They're mostly volunteers from last year's flowers, coming up on their own."

Apparently the volunteer plant army is being all it can be . . .

Friends, practical friends, engineer friends have tried to warn me off gardening altogether. "With the time and money invested, you're way better off just buying your produce from the store." People do wonder why we'd spend hard-earned money on garden tools that unfortunately fit our hands so that we can then engage in backbreaking work and come in at day's end all sweaty and with socks black around the ankles. And then my logical, practical, engineer friends wonder aloud why, at the very least, why I would be a willing accomplice to my wife's folly? —"Waste of time and money!"— I hear it again and again.

But it's a hobby. Last year we pulled in over 200 pounds, wheelbarrow loads, of winter squash (and I love the stuff) from our garden. The squash in our root cellar fed us and some friends too, clear into the next May. We buy vegetables only 12 weeks a year. No, not practical perhaps, but how many hobbies pay any dividend at all? I remember my sweetie laughing and saying that spaghetti squash is $1.79 a pound at the market. "We're squash millionaires!" was her laughter-filled observation.

Thinking of my very practical friends, none of whom garden, I am reminded of an old saying about folks who know the cost of everything and the value of nothing. The simple and biggest reason that I am a willing accomplice in the garden is that it makes her happy.

She bursts through the door in her huge sun hat, a rose blush to her tanned cheeks and grinning from ear to ear. "Have you seen the peas today?" she asks, and, "The corn is as high as an elephant's eye! Come! Come see!" She takes my hand and together we step out into late summer golden evening light to survey our garden and its eager, optimistic, and leaping growth . . .

Evenings on the ranch become chilly as darkness comes sooner with autumn. Then one night there's a touch of frost and the squash vine's leaves collapse like damp tissue paper. We let our squash turn a deep golden yellow on the vines and before the nights become too cold, and we harvest them all. Ultimately even our hardiest plants succumb to the encroaching, inexorable icy breath of winter.

Daylight grows short and winter is with us in earnest. Caught in icy winds, trees naked and skeletal beat their knobby, sere branches against our west windows. Wind moans around the house and snow crystals pile up in drifts on the deck where once, in our memory of longer days, we sat taking it all in, drinking tea and breathing fragrant warm evening air.

> "Daylight grows short and winter is with us in earnest. Caught in icy winds, trees naked and skeletal beat their knobby, sere branches against our west windows."

Winter wears on at the ranch. I come in from feeding and breaking the ice off the animal's water with chapped cold cheeks and a frigid dripping nose. Shucking snowy boots, I pad over and do the wood stove hug, closely encircling but not touching the hot stove pipe. Water sizzles as the snow melts off of me and patters onto the stove top. Warmed but still damp, I sit for dinner. The wind rises and our stove pipe shudders. In pitch blackness snow hisses against dark window panes.

Smiling proudly, she sets it all before me. Our beloved squash, bursting with flavor, awaits my fork. I smile up at her smiling down. Before I even touch the chicken, I dig my fork into a hot, sweet and buttery mound. —Of summer. ❁

Perfect Eggs

by Sylvia Woods

Should come from happy hens,
dams who roam free,
eat as they please,
consort with roosters
they pick themselves.
Gorged on sex and freedom
they lay eggs so rich
they glisten on the plate.

"Spring Break" by Robin Peterson

A Tale of Two Birds
The Creature Feature by DB Rudin

Drawing by R. Bruce Horsfall
MAGPIE
A mixture of shyness and boldness

Photo by W. L. Finley and H. T. Bohlman
RUFOUS HUMMINGBIRD

Unbidden or invited, birds visit our gardens and our lives. They live in our songs and stories and are harbingers of change as they set off on great journeys of migration. I created a homemade waterfall in my backyard. Birds, butterflies, squirrels, dogs, and dragonflies are all regular visitors. So far, in three and a half years, forty-two species of birds have paid a visit. Here are two of their stories.

Not every bird visiting the backyard garden is the bluebird of happiness, and perhaps no one group of birds sizes us up as suckers better than the *Corvidae*, that family of genius malcontents watching us and our habits while we blithely go about our daily lives. Ravens, crows, jays, and magpies form quite the formidable group of avian rebels. They eat seemingly anything, and they can live anywhere, often because of the food found around human dwellings in places like gardens and trash.

No other bird visitor cases the joint quite like the magpies. The black-billed magpie (*Pica hudsonia*) is the long-tailed, black-and-white, crow-like bird of the western U. S. Their squawking is a regular feature of the landscape, an unconscious reminder of place. While we easily ignore them, they watch us closely. In Native American legend they embody sharp eyes, wisdom, and a bit of the trickster.

I don't remember the exact date when a group of magpies first showed up in the backyard. I do remember that the baby green tomatoes disappeared soon thereafter. They had been growing in a pot on the back porch and then they were gone. No cold, hard evidence as to the culprit, yet there were those magpies.

Two innocuous garter snakes had taken up a life of leisure sunning amongst the rocks of the backyard waterfall, chasing after baby goldfish in the deep pool below and avoiding humans. They relaxed over time and humans were eventually seen as a merely unpleasant interruption in their sunbathing routine and eventually ignored. Apparently that was a poor choice of strategies when encountering the magpies, as one half-eaten snake later proved. The second snake was never seen again.

I would have spotted the magpies that much, but when they ate the blooms on the scarlet begonias they crossed the line. This seemed less like hustling a meal and more like wanton vandalism. While birds certainly do eat flowers, my relationship with the magpies took on a decidedly adversarial tone after that. As the summer wore on, the battle was to save some of the ripening tomatoes that they missed the first time. (I can't imagine they missed them, I think they were letting them ripen.) While they lurk out back feigning disinterest and missing nothing, I'm plotting my tomato coup. I plan on eating those tomatoes. Despite my resolve, the Vegas Line would probably have the smart money on the magpies.

On the other end of the charm scale, hummingbirds give off their own distinctive vibe. Nothing says "easy living" like hummingbirds sipping nectar in the mid-summer garden. These little colored jewels can be seemingly capricious in choosing whether to patronize one's establishment, but a little sugar water or flower nectar and some cover is usually enough to entice these flying acrobats.

Be forewarned if you decide to put out a feeder to tempt them to visit your backyard; hummingbirds aren't all sweetness and light. They are known to be a little full of themselves and can treat humans like somewhat dim servants. Keepers of hummingbird feeders regularly tell of hummingbirds buzzing around their heads and sometimes flying through open doors or windows to let humans know the feeders are empty.

When not ordering around humans, hummingbirds live life on the edge. They seem to always be going a million miles an hour. Actually they are routinely going north of 1,200 heartbeats per minute and can dive at 60 mph, all the while going in any direction in three dimensions. Yet, these high powered flying machines weigh less than a penny when born.

Aeronautical mastery is essential, but so are other skills such as timing, especially on long migration routes. Rufous hummingbirds (*Selasphorus rufus*) are as notorious for their aggressive, feeder-dominating temperaments as their long distance migrations. These journeys can go all the way from central Mexico to Alaska, about 2,700 miles one way. To do this, they might break their trip into as many as four segments. Each stopover site is critical for refueling. Routes might be changed from year to year due to availability of nectar-producing plants like the octotillo (*Fouquieria splendens*) in the Sonoran Desert. There is evidence to suggest that they remember sites from year to year. An exhausted bird arriving at a previously productive spot that's been turned into a housing development for example, can spell disaster. The margin for mishaps is razor thin.

For some hummingbirds, migration requires crossing barriers that are all or nothing. Every fall, first-year Ruby-Throated hummingbirds (*Archilochus colubris*) of the eastern United States face a journey that would make Lucky Lindy blanch. They take a literal leap into the unknown, completely based on something more primal than faith . . . instinct.

In preparing for their epic journey they enter into a state scientists refer to as hyperphagia, the mother of all attack-of-the-munchies. In fact, these birds can double their weight, laid on mostly as fat. These somewhat stouter hummingbirds travel to the north shore of the Gulf of Mexico and wait for favorable winds. Tail winds, usually following a cold front, can greatly ease the journey, and it taxes the fat reserves far less. A head wind can mean perishing at sea. This is a journey with no forgiveness for not finishing: 500 miles across the Gulf of Mexico, non-stop, alone, much of it in the dark. Oh, and they've never done it before. They are relying totally on an instinctual map as their elders have already gone ahead. It is a voyage beyond human conception.

> " . . . hummingbirds aren't all sweetness and light. They are known to be a little full of themselves and can treat humans like somewhat dim servants."

Aside from a little maintenance, my backyard waterfall takes little and delivers a lot. For me, spring is spring only when I've seen the first male Western Tanager (*Piranga ludoviciana*) fiery red, yellow, black and white, stopping by for a drink and a bath on its way to nest in conifer forests. And in the fall, when the last of the migrants (last year a gray catbird, *Dumatella carolinensis*) passes through in late October or early November, I know winter is around the corner.

In contrast to the epic journeys of migration, my preparation for winter consists of little beyond mulching the garden, getting some firewood, and breaking out the warm clothes. The magpies will stay, eeking out an existence with their smarts and adaptability. The hummingbirds, on the other hand . . . well, I'll think of them on those long, dark nights of winter as I imagine the return of the golden days of summer and summer's sparkling muses. ✽

Author's Note: Final Tomato Score: Humans: 6; Magpies: several dozen.

En Route
by Amanda Laughtland

I'm driving since the bed of Trish's pickup
is too cold for the bees and its cab
too close for me. Their box

rests in my trunk, just past
the lowered back seat and well within
Trish's reach if she turns and leans

and stretches her arms at full length.
Pressing close to their queen
ten thousand bees don't buzz at all

until a car stops short
and I have to brake quickly,
toppling the bees and spilling their can

of sugar syrup. The buzzing is only
static, I tell myself, static
from a little talk radio station
broadcasting from fifty miles away.

"Bees in the Barn" by Jill Bates

Chamomile Tea

Trish steeps dry, golden flowers
in sugary water for the colony
who use their time and energy
making wax. It's too cold for California bees

to find pollen in their new city
and their hive needs comb. Bees take tea
with local honey. They take it a little
alkaline, just over a seven. Trish tests

and retests the pH with a paper strip
and finishes with the juice of one lemon.

Amy's Other Art

An Interview with Amy Stewart

by Jennifer Newcomb Marine

Photo by Scott Brown

Amy Stewart is the author of five books on the natural world, including three New York Times bestsellers: *Flower Confidential*, *Wicked Plants*, and *Wicked Bugs*. Her earlier two were *From the Ground Up* (a memoir on her first garden) and *The Earth Moved* (about earthworms). She has also written a novel, *The Last Bookstore in America*. She's a writer, a gardener, and a lover of cocktails. (I can hardly wait to read her upcoming book, *The Drunken Botanist: The Plants that Create the World's Best Drinks*, coming this spring.) Like many highly creative types, it doesn't stop there. She has also been painting for ten years. In this interview, originally published in *Daily Paintworks*, Stewart talks about her visual art. —*Editor*

Tell us a bit about how you first started painting.

I grew up in a family of painters—my mother and my brother—but I never painted. I always thought that art was their thing. Then, in my twenties, I got the idea that it would be fun to learn to draw a little, just enough to maybe scribble in a travel journal or draw little pictures in my garden. When I was 30, my husband and I quit our jobs, moved to Eureka, CA, and became self-employed. (I'm a writer and he's a bookseller.) So I had some time on my hands and I started looking around for a drawing class to take.

I did a couple of short-term classes, and when those ended, the only other thing that really worked with my schedule was an oil painting class with a painter whose work I really loved. (Linda Mitchell, who has also joined Daily Paintworks.) I didn't think I would like oil painting—it sounded so complicated compared to scribbling in a journal with a pen—but it turned out that I loved it. Painting in oils is very much like writing—it's all about revision. I'm so used to editing, rewriting, throwing things away that don't work. When Linda says, "You need to wipe that out and start over," I just shrug and go, "Okay." Doesn't bother me at all. I do it all the time as a writer.

So I'm still in that class, 10 years later. It's become more like a social hour—a bunch of women who get together to paint, drink wine, and gossip once a week.

What sort of art do you love to do?

Well, oils, definitely. And I work from photographs, because cities don't sit still long enough to paint them from life. Cityscapes are by far my favorite subject, and New York is my favorite city. I don't do touristy things when I travel—I'm very happy to just pick a neighborhood and spend all day walking around, taking pictures.

And there is a particular kind of cityscape I seem to paint over and over again, which is a long view down a busy street, looking into the distance. I just love that feeling of the buildings rising up into the sky and people and cars rushing around, and the possibility of something interesting at the end of that street. And I love that moment with the lights come up in the early evening. That's my favorite time to walk around and take pictures—starting an hour or two before sunset, and continuing until it's too dark to get a good photograph.

I have a few other specific things that I love to paint. It's funny—if you'd asked me before I started painting, I probably would have said that a good painter learns to do everything equally well. I had a friend who only painted fish and olives. Fish and olives! That's crazy! But I kind of get it now. Certain subjects are just fun to paint, and interesting, and if a painter figures out a way to do it that no one else is doing, why not run with it?

So I love to paint chickens—I have a little flock in my backyard and they pose for me—but I treat them like serious portraits, with these dark grey Sears Portrait Studio type backgrounds. And I love to paint the insides of bars—I like low light, and the bottles, and the dark figures. I do still life from time to time, when the farmer's market is particularly inspiring. I learned a lot about still life from a workshop with Carol Marine a few years ago.

I have been terrible about learning to paint figures and particularly faces. I took Karin Jurick's workshop in New York because I wanted to get better about putting figures into my cityscapes. I'd always thought of Karin as a painter of city-

Lunch at the New York Public Library by Amy Stewart

scapes, but of course she's a painter of people. Sometimes those people happen to be in a city. So I really learned from her to approach it differently—rather than find an interesting street and stand there until I could get a good photo, I learned to pick an interesting-looking person and follow them around until the light hit them just right or I liked their pose.

But I'm still totally intimidated by it and I revert to these busy streetscapes with tiny little wisps of figures off in the distance. Or I paint people only from behind so I don't have to deal with their faces. It's funny—look at my paintings and how no one is ever looking at the camera!

Did you have any stops and starts in your painting career?

One of the great joys for me about painting is that I'm not obligated to think about it as a career. I have a difficult career in the arts already! I don't need another one. So I paint, and of course I sell the paintings because I don't want hundreds of little paintings sitting around the house, but I don't feel obligated to build a resume or anything like that. I turn down commissions—I tell people that I take "requests" and that if it works out, they can have first right of refusal, but no commissions!

And I never enter contests or apply for awards—why would I? It won't make me a better painter, and that's all I'm really interested in. I don't even really want to do gallery shows. I agreed to do a local show in December, but only because I know it will be the easiest thing in the world for me to put 20 paintings in the car and take them down there. If it was going to be any more complicated than that, I would have passed. I get a ridiculous amount of satisfaction from selling a little painting to a complete stranger on DPW and packing that up and shipping it off. That, to me, is as much of the trappings of a "career" as I want.

Chickens!

What mediums and genres have you experimented with? Which ones have "stuck" and which ones have fallen away? Which ones are you looking forward to exploring?

I took a charcoal drawing class, and while I learned a lot, all that charcoal dust got tiresome. The medium just didn't appeal. I have a little portable watercolor set and I'll do watercolor washes over a pen drawing when I'm traveling, but that's just for fun. I've played around with acrylics when I'm painting with my friends' kids, but I don't really understand how they work so I end up frustrated if I'm trying to do anything more than join the five year-olds in splattering paint around. Really, I think oils are it for me.

I would like to paint bigger, but then the question becomes—what do I do with all those big paintings? Little paintings are so easy to sell online, and if one doesn't work out, I don't have much invested in it and I can just move on. But I would like to work big, and several painters whose work I admire have told me I'll learn a lot if I'll just go big for a while.

What does procrastination look like for you? What techniques work to ensure that you make time for your art?

I am so very relieved that I never feel like I have to paint. Painting is the thing I can't wait to have more time to do. I still go to my painting class on Wednesday nights, and unless I'm out of town, I never, ever miss it. Beyond that, it's just a joy for me to find that I have enough time in the day to paint.

Once in a while I'll find myself with time to paint, but I'm not really in the mood. When that happens, I just go over to my little painting space and start gessoing some boards. Karin Jurick taught me to paint on black gesso, which I adore. It makes the colors pop in this extraordinary way. And sometimes I'll use acrylic paint, maybe a crazy orange or green, as a ground. So there's always a little gesso work to be done, and usually by the time I have a brush out and I'm putting paint on something, I'm in the mood to paint again.

What do you feel you are learning about right now as an artist?

Well, I think I'm getting a little more accurate and detailed and tight, and for me, that's a good thing. I'll hear some painters say, "Oh, I'm trying not to be so tight, I really need to loosen up," and I think, "Wow, I just can't paint with any precision. I don't know how." Or, more to the point, I don't know how to do it in a short period

Ladybird

of time, and because of my busy schedule, I want to be able to do a small painting in a short period of time and actually finish it. So I'm learning how to be a little tighter and more accurate but still be pretty fast.

And I am trying to get better with figures—but then I think, "Why? Who says I have to get better with figures? Is somebody going to give me a bad grade if I don't? Am I going to get fired?"

(And since you're also a writer…) Any differences in your creative approach between writing and art?

Oh, everything. As a writer, I have to think all the time about what will sell, what will appeal to a broad audience, how to market myself—all of that. I get to paint just to please me. They are miles and miles apart. One of the best differences between the two is that I get to paint standing up, away from a computer (OK, I use my iPad for my photo references), while listening to music and possibly drinking a nice cocktail. I do not have to wrestle with words—I can put my hyper-verbal brain in neutral and (sort of) think about nothing. Bliss!

Having said that, there are so many weird parallels between writing and painting. I sometimes think about teaching a workshop about that—I have a long list of all the surprising similarities. One in particular is that there is a narrative quality to painting. It took me years to realize this—in fact, it only came to me last year. I was working on this evening streetscape from a photo I took in my neighborhood. The camera was slightly tilted, everything was a little out of focus, and you could see the neighborhood but you could also see, at the very end of the street, the little lights of the bars downtown. I thought, "This is a painting of someone stumbling home drunk! This is what they see." It's the first time I really thought about the fact that a painting is seen through someone's eyes, and that someone is like a narrator or a character in a story.

I'm always telling my writing students that even if they are not writing in the first person, they are still present in the story as a narrator. What they chose to say and not to say, and how they say it, tells the reader something about them, and in that way they become a character. That's true in painting, too. A cityscape is a perspective on a city seen through someone's eyes. I just put up a painting on DPW of an alley in the French

Quarter and I look at that painting and think, "That is a scene. It's a scene in someone's life, in some story." I don't mean that literally, as in, "Well, this is Katy, and she's just getting off from her first day at work…" but in a more vague sense, it feels full of narrative possibilities.

What makes you happiest about your art?

I love doing something consistently, over many years, and doing it reasonably well, but with no attachment to the outcome or to any definition of success. When I read some great book by a writer I admire, all I can think about is whether I will or will not ever be able to do anything like that. But I go to a gallery or a museum to look at paintings, and I never get that feeling that I need to catch up with them or compete. It's great.

And I love thinking about the possibility of painting more. I would like nothing more than to be able to go to some interesting city for a month and paint there, sell the paintings, and somehow finance one adventure after another that way. That's not very realistic, but I love thinking about it.

I think all writers envy painters—one of my favorite writers, Geoff Dyer, said this in his book *Out of Sheer Rage*:

"For the painter work means a more intense physical engagement with life, it begins with carpentry (making stretchers) and ends in glazing, varnishing, and framing . . . In the age of the computer the writer's office or study will increasingly resemble the customer service desk of an ailing small business."

So I'm very happy that painting lets me get away from my "ailing small business" and go have some fun!

Thanks so much, Amy! ✳

Egg-shell experiment farm. The plants from left to right:
cabbage, field corn, popcorn, wheat, buckwheat.

From *Handbook of Nature Study*, 1947.

Rockstars of Biology

(Match the man to his Magnificent Obsession)

1. Born at South Råshult, Sweden, 1707; died at Upsala, 1778.
Author of the first comprehensive system of classification of plants.

2. Born at Warsaw, 1844; died at Bonn, 1912.
Founder of the study of the structure and functions of living plant cells.

3. Born at Breslau, 1832; died at Würzburg, 1897.
Contributed greatly to the development of experimental methods, which he used in studying photosynthesis, starch-formation, respiration, and the relations of plants to water.

4. Born at Dôle, France, 1822; died at St. Cloud, 1895. The most important contributor to the study of bacteria and yeasts, especially in their relations to man.

5. Born at Heinzendorf, 1822; died at Brünn, 1884. Developed the method, now everywhere in use, of studying inheritance by means of crosses between parents differing in one or more characters.

6. Born at Shrewsbury, England, 1809; died at Down, 1882.
First established upon a firm basis the theory of the origin of species by descent.

A. Edward Strasburger

B. Charles Darwin

C. Carl Von Linné (Linnaeus)

D. Louis Pasteur

E. Julius Sachs

F. Gregor Mendel

Answers: 1. C, 2. A, 3. E, 4. D, 5. F, 6. B

Greenwoman Magazine

Escape to the garden.

Deputy Editor Zora Knauf, with her sidekick Chancho, at **Greenwoman**'s Vermijo Community Garden plot, September 2012. *Photo by Paul Spielman.*

Radish Gets Around

by Mae Fayne & Angus Skillet

Last year it was Rob Radish. "I'm in LOVE!" she told me.

A month after she broke up with Rob, Gerald Green Pepper declared *his* love! (That didn't last either.)

Then it was Sam Squash!

She comes running back to me . . . and I always take her back.

FernWood studio

Robin Peterson

www.fernwoodstudio.com
info@fernwoodstudio.com

prints
originals
greeting cards
wedding invitations
commissioned projects

ZOË TILLEY POSTER

fine art and illustration

zoeposter.com

dailypaintworks.com

Browse over 62,000 paintings, including floral & garden. Find or commission the perfect collection for your home.

Want a Backyard Farm?

RIGHT TO THRIVE

Backyard Farming on the Front Range

RightToThrive.org
Designs • DIY Plans • Classes
Christine Faith 719.448.0885

DOUBLE AND SINGLE HYACINTH.
1. NOBLE PAR MERITE.   2 GRAND LILAC

Illustration from *The Graphics Fairy* (http://www.thegraphicsfairy.com)

Grow

by Carolyn Williams-Noren

Get bigger, of course.
Spread thinner. Split
open. Let some parts
die. Fill the hollow at
your center. Make seeds,
and drop them. Risk
being eaten alive. Take
what you need. Weep
for water. Grab onto
what's nearby. Leave
behind neatness. Press
yourself open—uncurl
your spine. Divide.

PAT KENNELLY

CREATIVE COPY FOR COMPANY WEBSITES & BLOGS

Pat is an experienced writer and blogger, who specializes in food, gardening, business and travel writing. Please see her blog at http://writingnag.com

PUBLICATIONS INCLUDE:
Denver Post, Articus, Irish American Post, Artella, Springs Magazine and Haibun Today.

PAT KENNELLY • 719-466-1149

Rhonda Van Pelt

editor, writer, graphic designer, artist and nature lover

I can polish your words and turn them into

a work of art.

And my rates are reasonable, too!

rhonda.vanpelt@comcast.net

NH4W.com
Natural Health 4 Wellness
NaturalHealth4Wellness.com

INDEPENDENT DISTRIBUTOR

Save Up To 45% OFF Retail Price

600+ Natural Health Products for:
- Dry & Problem Skin
- Allergy & Sinus Relief
- Cleanse & Detox
- Herbal Supplements
- Nutritional Supplements
- Flower Essences (liquid extracts)
- Essential Oils (aromatherapy)
- Natural Weight Loss
- Vitamins & Minerals
- Sleep & Insomnia Products
- Anxiety & Stress Relief
- Childrens Supplements
- Women's Health Products
- Men's Health Products
- Natural Energy Drinks
- Body System Packs
- ... *And MORE!*

We Make Living Healthy Fun!
* FREE Spa & Wellness Parties
* Personalized Wellness Assessments
* FREE Natural Health Classes

Enter Our Contest!
Join our mailing list to enter

TAKE TO THE HILLS

AN OZARK CHRONICLE

by *Marguerite Lyon*

"MARGE OF SUNRISE MOUNTAIN FARM"

Cover art and illustration by Ronald Bean

Editor's Note: Years ago I came across one of Marguerite Lyon's books, *And Green Grass Grows All Around*, on my neighborhood library "Friends" sale bookshelf for $1. I saw that the publication date was 1942 and opened the book to a random page. Soon I was deep into an account of Marge running around in the middle of the night looking for a good set of sheets for her guest bed. She had returned home from a trip to find unexpected visitors, a couple her husband ("The Jedge") had married. The problem? Her linens had been the victim of an "Ozark trade," surreptitiously exchanged on the clothesline for some burlap-rough, patched, fraction-of-the-size sheets. Lyon's humor and fine writing (she worked in advertising in Chicago in the 1930s) hooked me. It was especially delightful to discover that the stories she told were about people who were probably my own "kin," those of Scots-Irish heritage who settled in the Ozarks around the area of Mountain View, Missouri.

Several of her books are now available as free downloads from the Internet Library and we plan to republish three of Lyon's books in 2014 in paperback. It's a joy to share with you the introduction and first chapter from her first book about Sunrise Mountain Farm, *Take to the Hills.—Sandra Knauf*

From the Introduction

HAVE YOU EVER WANTED A FARM?

YOUR answer to that question, I am sure, is yes! In fact, the Jedge and I have come to believe that America is made up of two classes of people, those who want a big farm, and those who want just any kind of a farm.

Throughout the five years that we have owned Sunrise Mountain Farm, we have been amazed at the number of people who had a farm urge! The butcher, baker, doorman, window-washer, banker, taxi-driver . . all had that yearning for a place in the country.

Their reasons for wanting a farm gave us endless amusement: A place to putter with flowers. Nearer to a golf course. More space for the children to play. A place to keep a dog. Better air! Fresh eggs.

We had to answer the oddest questions, too.

Did we have movies near us? Could we get good help? Did we have electricity? Were the roads good? It seemed to us that everyone wanted a farm without foregoing any of the urban luxuries.

Suddenly, within the past year, these questions have taken a more serious turn! With the world rocking on its heels, with the very air filled with talk of decentralizing population, rumors of mysterious attacks, and vague internal and international complications, people seem to be turning to Mother Earth as the only real, substantial thing left to humanity.

Now we are asked what one feeds a cow, how many eggs each day does a hen lay, and what sort of income crops one could plant on a farm. The Man on the Street now seems to feel that a farm is the only genuine security if . . . well, if Things get Worse.

This book is not intended to present this matter of city-folks-going-to-the-country in an authoritative manner. Every family has its personal problems that must be worked out in an individual manner, whether it be in the city or on a farm. It just happens that the Ozarks suit us . . . and we get a kick out of talking about our farm in the hills.

Ronnie Bean, who has drawn the pictures, spent considerable time at our farm before he drew so much as a blade of grass. Even the whiskers are authentic.

What you will read in this book you have my word is the absolute truth. Down here in the hills, truth may not be stranger than fiction, but in many instances it's a lot funnier! That's why we'll **TAKE TO THE HILLS.**

Chapter One

FIRE ON THE MOUNTAIN

FLAMES race to the top of the great pine tree at the southeast corner of Sunrise Mountain Farm, making it a fiery torch. Then, topped by towering twisting clouds of smoke, a wall of fire moves into the thick underbrush at the base of the tree and comes on with terrifying intent. The tall sassafras pole, topped with a fluttering striped pennant that marks the sixth hole of our golf course, burns like a kindling splinter.

What we have so greatly feared has come upon us. Forest fire!

It is the law of the hills here in the Ozarks that farmers notify their neighbors before they begin to burn off the tall dry grass and dead leaves prior to the spring growing season. But we have had no such warning. Perhaps the fire has escaped from the control of a far-distant farmer. Perhaps it was started by someone who does not care what happens to the other fellow's farm. But this is no time to wonder where this fire originated. It is here on Sunrise Mountain Farm! And it is up to us to save our buildings and livestock.

With feed bags sopped in pails of pond water, we flail with might and main at the flames as they creep into the clearing of the forty acres on which our home and main outbuildings are located. Tongues of flame are moving across the clearing that serves as golf course, sheep pasture, picnic ground, and our evening sitting-out place. To me, they seem like great fingers, tipped with blood-red claws, grappling onward, clutching and crumbling dry feathery grasses, brittle seed pods, and the brown, tinder-dry leaves of the jack-oak clumps. The roar of the fire is as the roar of a cyclone. Flying sparks sting and burn. Smoke hides the morning sun and burns our eyes. On moves the fire, faster than a walking pace, over a mile-wide front.

So swiftly have the flames come through the forests south and east of our farm that even the guinea hen, that inveterate fraidy-cat, gave us no warning. She's making up for lost time now! The geese are honking and hissing at our feverish activity. Hens are cackling nervously. We scream at one another above the roar of the flames.

"There's another pail in the cave-house!"

"You'll find more feed bags in that hamper in the pantry!"

Then we fall silent, working desperately to fight back the flames.

We have no fire equipment. But even the best equipment would be useless without more water and man power. We have no hose and no way of getting water through it. At Sunrise Mountain we have only a hand pump in our big well and a windlass in our cistern. The water, even in these early spring days, is limited in quantity. For our fire department we have only the Jedge, now hoarsely shouting commands, Roy, our faithful hired man, Willard Jones, who happened to be here cutting wood, and myself.

At last we abandon the flailing. We find the flames creeping beyond us at unprotected points! We race back to

"I want to scream, to weep, to rage at fate. We've worked so hard for our farm. Must we see our buildings ruined by fire here on this sunny March morning?"

the buildings at the top of the hill, flames snapping at our heels and sending stinging sparks ahead to taunt us. The Jedge looks the situation over! I know he is seeing, as I do, that the barns, with the wide sheep wings extending at each side, will be the first to go, if, or when, the flames reach the hilltop. Twenty feet from the corral fence he puts a lighted match into the dry grass. It is the start of our backfire that will, like a tiny David, go out to meet the Goliath of flames now racing up the hillside.

Already the fire has leaped the rocky ravine and moved on to the giant hickory tree that grows the biggest hickory nuts in the Ozark Mountains. We see the sputtering sparks in the pall of smoke, where hundreds of dry nuts, left under the trees for the squirrels, are now burning. We see the flames move on and ignite the protecting fence around the hotbed. Roy rushes to put a pail of our precious water on it and comes back nursing a scorched hand. He has worked so hard to grow tomato plants bigger and better than any others in the hills. His "incubator babies," we have called them. Now their incubator is a seething inferno. Soon the fire will reach the outdoor fireplace. I measure the distance with my eyes and know it must be stopped here! . . . Or else! . . .

The backfire moves onward. The men watch for even the tiniest flame that dares to burn backward toward the corral fence and pounce on it with moistened feed bag.

I want to scream, to weep, to rage at fate. We've worked so hard for our farm. Must we see our buildings ruined by fire here on this sunny March morning? But this is no time for heroics. The Jedge is shouting my orders. Get the car out of the garage! Load it with things we will need if we have to abandon the house! (Oh, dear God, surely our house won't go!) Put the dogs in the dining room, where we can get them instantly. Where's the cat? Put her in the pantry. Bring out bedclothes! Sop them in the pond and hang them on the wooden fences.

I obey as in a trance! The dogs and cat come first . . . they are soon inside the house. I understand why the Jedge had told me to put them in definite rooms, instead of allowing them to roam through the house as always. In a last moment of panic, they might hide under beds or in corners where they would be difficult to find.

As I put the cat in the pantry, I look for a moment from the breakfast nook windows. The rolling billows of smoke have taken on new fury! Now they have moved into our

That which we have so greatly feared . . .

scenic Stone Terrace Hill, the home of myriads of soft, feathery and furry wild things that have lived secure under our protection these past four years.

I suddenly recall the saucy little fox that had trotted into those woods with a flick of his bushy tail toward me and the dogs and a N'ya N'ya look on his bright little face long before Kay Kyser put the words into his mouth. I remember the soft baby quail that had flown directly to the Jedge's finger in a startled moment, and each had looked at the other with the same wonderment, I think of the possums which climbed the twin persimmon trees at the edge of the clearing each frosty night last autumn, leaving sleekly polished seeds, bright as varnished mahogany, under the trees as a remembrance of their feast. Are they racing, all these little wild things, with their pounding hearts and stricken eyes, before that wall of flame?

"Hurry with those bedclothes!" shouts the Jedge.

"Bring out the stuff you would want to take with you! Leave the car at the back gate! I'm going for the sheep! If the whole farm burns, we can drive them out on the highway."

"Without a qualm, I tear from beds and chests the treasured patchwork quilts made by my mother and grandmother. Moth balls scatter over the floor like white marbles as I bring out precious hand-quilted satin comforters filled with fine white wool from our own sheep. Out, too, come fleecy blankets in pastel colors, relics of pre-depression days, Roy comes in, grimy and smoke-blackened, to help carry them out. Soon they hang sopping, with muddy pond water dripping from satin bindings and handmade borders, on the corral fence and the gates,

In the distance, I hear the Jedge calling the sheep. Or rather, one sheep. Alice! Alice was a bottle-raised lamb and still answers our call! If she comes, the others will follow.

Loading the car for fleeing is another matter. What, I wonder, does a refugee take? For an instant, I know something of the agony of civilians in warring countries. I, too, have the heartbreak that comes from parting with beloved possessions, the terror of an uncertain future. I rush aimlessly from room to room. They are so bright and clean, so carefully tended. Only an hour ago, I suddenly recall, I was terribly concerned over the warp of that living room wood box lid. In another hour . . . but I refuse to think even for a moment what might be in store for this house.

In a fury of activity, I seize heavy coats and shoes and stack them on the floor in the kitchen. Sweaters, leather jackets, wool socks go into the pile. I try to think of other

A delightful
gift
for
the Holidays
or any special occasion.

Greenwoman
Magazine

Antique image from TheGraphicsFairy.com

essentials. My best dress . . . those silk stockings out of that drawer . . . the Jedge's newest suit . . . and that old brown flannel suit he loves so dearly. I can't take much. We must leave room in the car for the dogs and cat.

The Jedge's steel file cabinet comes next. This, too, must go with us! I wonder about our deeds, our insurance papers! Are they in our safety deposit box at the bank in the village? Why are people so careless about such things? I resolve never again to be so negligent.

As I pass through the living room, planned to meet our own particular needs, I grab from the long china shelves a single red plate. Surely one sentimental gesture is permissible. We started housekeeping with that bright red tea set, unpacking two of these plates from their original wrappings of Chinese newspapers, for the first meal in our new home. I put the plate in the front seat of the car when I take out the next load of clothing.

On my way back to the house, I pick up Ronnie and Barbara, the pet Bantams, and put them with the dogs in the dining room. They are too little, too defenseless, to be left in the path of the flame.

> "Hour after hour goes by. Time and Food are forgotten . . . Pailful after pailful is carried through tangled thickets of wild blackberry bushes and up rocky hillsides, crossed and crisscrossed with narrow sheep trails!"

Judy is shivering in the warm room. It is the first time I have ever seen this stout-hearted little Boston terrier frightened. Punch, the shepherd, has his head in a corner, his usual thunderstorm position. I shut the door to keep out as much of the smoke as possible and go back to the backfire.

The Jedge is bringing up the sheep, with Alice in the lead, the tinkling bell at her throat a strangely peaceful note in this unpeaceful hour. Roy hurries to close the east gate of the lane before the sheep get to it. Robert (he is my husband and the Jedge I've been talking about) closes the west gate when the last straggler has been hustled inside, and the sheep are left in their narrow smoky haven, milling about and baa-ing reproaches.

With parched lips, aching throats, and blackened faces streaked with tears, we fight to keep the backfire moving forward. At last, a stone's throw from the corral fences and the honeysuckle-covered arch of the backyard fence, it meets the oncoming wall of flame, and, . . thank God ... It holds. Unless the fire comes from another front, we have saved our barn and house.

But only a moment of respite we know. The fire moves on the Saunders farm north of us, skirting the big pond and barely missing the tiny building that houses the geese. Then long fingers of flame begin to creep through the grass toward the new jelly kitchen on the hilltop.

Another backfire must be built. Again we flail desperately to keep it from creeping back toward the building it was meant to save. Again the bedding is dipped in the pond and swathed over the end of the building, like a badly arranged booth at a church bazaar. We watch the flames roll through our struggling young orchard . . . the orchard bought with the money I earned teaching in night school one whole winter in Chicago. Then the fire sweeps on to wriggle like a flaming serpent along the stake-and-rider rail fence at the Saunders farm. But again, a stone's throw from the new building, our backfire meets the wall of flame and holds. Encouraged by two victories, we turn to the third front, the southern boundary of our farm.

Thank goodness, our long vegetable garden is barren of rubbish, ready for the plow! It is our line of defense on the south. But the flames have now reached the forty acres adjoining our Home Forty on the west. We must protect the house from that direction. The fire sweeps through the dry oak leaves. In another moment it will reach the valley west of us, We must save the cabin and other buildings acquired when we bought this forty-acre piece of land, known as the Arnold Forty. We need that big barn and corncrib! And we hope we shall need the funny little unoccupied cabin for many more honey-mooners, as we have needed it in the past. Backfires are hastily set and flailing is wearily begun.

Neighbors come at last to help us. Aunt Mealie Saunders, despite the misery in her knee, hurries down from her home to the north of us to see if the fire is likely to reach her home. She has left dear old Uncle Pete, convalescing from pneumonia, in that ramshackle little cabin which would burn like tinder. The Jedge calls to Willard Jones to take another man and go up to backfire around the Saunders' buildings. They hurry away, and we work all the harder to make up for them.

Hour after hour goes by. Time and food are forgotten. Fortunately, a forty-foot stock well and shallow pond near the cabin in the valley hold water for sopping the feed bags, with which we flail the flames. Pailful after pailful is carried through tangled thickets of wild blackberry bushes and up rocky hillsides, crossed and crisscrossed with narrow sheep trails! The spring, where clear, sparkling, icy water seeps into a twelve-foot rocky basin, becomes an added blessing when the well gives up its last drop!

There are many breath-taking incidents!

Once the outdoor toilet at the cabin catches fire. Roy races up with a pailful of water and dashes out most of the flame, kicking out the last tiny blaze on the charred corner with the toe of his dusty shoe.

It is impossible to stop the spread of the fire. It sweeps through the remainder of our land to the west. Then, late in the afternoon, a tall dead tree, flaming to its tip, falls across the road, carrying the fire to our North Forty. We see the flames scamper up the dry, grassy clearing on the hillside and head straight for the Saunders home beyond.

Our fire-fighting crew is now divided, half remaining to finish the job of protecting our buildings, the other half going up to save the Saunders home. Up there, the men and women (for women too have come to help us) must work in silence. There can be no loud shouting and calling as at our farm. Uncle Pete must not know his home is threatened.

The Jedge tells me to open the lane gates, so he can get the car through without letting the sheep out. He will take the car up the hill and keep it there in readiness for Uncle Pete if the Saunders house can't be saved. As I close the second gate behind him, he shouts orders about keeping the road clear of fallen trees, so he can get Uncle Pete back to our house. Through the breaks in the cloud of smoke, I see our clothes bouncing on the back seat as he hits the ruts on the hill. Those clothes will be a soft bed in the car for Uncle Pete, if the fire takes his home. But all our bedcovers, I suddenly remember, are still on the corral fences, smoke-stained and dripping wet.

The whole mountain is on fire. I think of the homes of neighbors in the path of the flames, which are sweeping northwest toward the river. None of these neighbors has come to help us. I know they are backfiring to save their homes. At least, I think thankfully, they have more warning of the fire than we had.

We seem to have been in this smoking, blazing furnace for a lifetime. We are bruised, scratched, ragged, grimy, and tired beyond words. But when a person is

> "We seem to have been in this smoking, blazing furnace for a lifetime. We are bruised, scratched, ragged, grimy, and tired beyond words. But when a person is fighting for the dearest thing in life, home, he cannot count the cost."

fighting for the dearest thing in life, home, he cannot count the cost. I lower another pail into the spring and haul up more water. Another fire fighter comes up and wearily takes it away.

At last, near ten o'clock at night, we can see that our buildings in the valley, as well as our home and buildings on the hilltop, are safe. The Saunders home, too, has been saved. Not by a miracle, but by the heroic, back-breaking work of our neighbors. Uncle Pete is told there is a fire in the distance, to explain the smoky air, and has gone peacefully to sleep. Roy takes the car to drive some of the fire fighters home. The Jedge and I stumble along the road toward home, the smoke hanging thickly about our heads in the chill quiet of the mountain night. The darkness of the countryside is punctured by hundreds o tiny fires . . . not friendly bonfires . . . but evil flames burning dead trees and down-timber that would have made honest, home-warming fires all winter. Every muscle aches, and bruises and scratches are beginning to make themselves felt under thick coats of smoky grime.

We release the dogs from their dining-room prison; the cat is brought from the pantry. The Bantams are detached from a rung on a Windsor chair and taken to the chicken house beside the barn. Before we prepare our own suppers, we go out to feed the sheep and put them in their corrals. There in the lane, among the crowded, frightened, bleating sheep, we find a tiny new lamb, born that day in the midst of sound and fury. He's a strong, sturdy little fellow, with a sooty black face and legs. We laugh . . . our first laugh in that awful day . . . and promptly name him Little Smoky.

Somehow Little Smoky brings us hope and courage. To us, he seems the symbol of Life in the midst of Death and Destruction. Or, perhaps, the promise of spring, gay, frisky, and carefree, after a winter of grief and anxiety. Spring will bring new life to our blackened trees and bald pastures. Spring will bring rain water in which I can wash my precious bedding, now so black and soiled. Spring may even help me forgive the person who started that fire. ❋

food

1. buy it with thought
2. cook it with care
3. use less wheat & meat
4. buy local foods
5. serve just enough
6. use what is left

don't waste it

U. S. FOOD ADMINISTRATION

Created by Frederic G. Cooper for the U. S. Food Administration, 1917.

Diary of A Garden Goddess

by Sandra Knauf

July 3, 2000

The first three hours working in the wealthy client's garden that hot morning are business as usual, focusing on the labors of weeding, watering, clipping, tying rose canes to arbors, all the while enjoying the sunshine and occasional refreshing mountain breeze.

Then boredom sets in. Because my daughters are young and I've been reading bushels of storybooks about talking animals, it seems natural to amuse myself by inventing tales about plants and other animated citizens of the garden.

I imagine the Kentucky Bluegrass family are the well-fed and manicured lords and ladies of the manor. And it's made them quite uppity.

"Oh, look, it's Mr. Dandelion," whispers Lady Grass to her friends, eyeing the stranger standing across the ballroom. "How did *he* get in here?" The ladies secretly think Mr. Dandelion dandy, a good-natured hunk with a gorgeous yellow mane. But he's not of "their kind," so they'd never say this aloud.

Lords Blade and Spike stand nearby. Blade smirks. "Oh, look Spike, it's Dandelion. You know how the Dandelions are—give them any room at all and they'll simply take over."

"Yes, and they are so garish! You know, I heard the Vincas are in the process of moving," says Spike. "They are quality, but still, it'll be nice to have the neighborhood to ourselves again."

The ladies overhear and smile at the lords. Everyone nods in approval.

I dig Mr. Dandelion out with my apple green Martha Stewart trowel. He takes it like a weed. Doesn't say a thing. "Sorry," I say, before tossing him next to the vincas I've dug out and potted.

In the hole created by Dandelion's departure I spy two worms. Even they are insufferable snobs.

"You're a Squiggle, son, act like it!" says Big Daddy Squiggles.

Sonny Boy Worm stretches tall, trying to make it appear that he has a spine.

Everyone knows their place here in the Broadmoor, our city's most monied, most pampered burg. The Broadmoor, home of the five-star, world famous hotel of the same name has been Colorado Springs' mecca of East Coast gentility since the town was founded in the once-wild 1860's West. It's nestled next to Cheyenne Mountain and the hotel has a new fence around it, just put in this year, to keep out the riff-raff. That would include me. I'm no one special. Just the hired help. A gardener.

I soon grow bored with the play, yet I'm still mostly content, deep in a blissful sun/work trance.

The spell vanishes when loud arguing comes from the mansion.

A male voice declares, "I only said I found her moderately attractive."

The female's reply is garbled.

Who are they talking about? I guess someone along the lines of a secretary, and I am uneasy to hear a domestic row. Then I imagine that perhaps the argument's about me. After all, there I crouch, easily visible not ten feet away from their huge Palladian-style windows, trimmed down and toned considerably from weeks of physical labor, brown as a berry, healthy, flushed with sweat and sunshine, feeling creative and a little sexy and interminably bored. Perhaps, I muse, my cleavage is visible as I tend the grass. Maybe the Mr. has a wondering eye, and the Mrs. is quite fed up with it.

My mind drifts again. I think about the film *Gods and Monsters* and how the gay director of *Frankenstein* fame lusted after Clay, or "the yard man," as he was called, played by Brendan Fraser. The old tomcat watched Clay from his window, greedily lapping him up visually like so much yardman/gardener cream. Soon Clay is invited in for a glass of iced tea, then lunch, then receives an offer for a modeling job, posing nearly nude (surprise!) for a painting.

My lingering bit of zen fades. I begin to feel as trapped as the yard man did, but in another way. I miss my girls, who are home with Andy, my self-employed husband. I'm tired of working out in this heat every day, waiting for my skin to shrivel up like a dried peach. My own garden's now seriously neglected, and I have an idea for a novel that's begging to get out on paper. I'm sick of working in spoiled rich people's gardens. Who am I kidding? Here I am, amusing myself by having

"A Garden Daydream" by Laura Chilson

the plants perform, by making up sexy gardener scenarios. I'm bored out of my freaking mind. I have been almost since I started this work.

* * *

For a few months I've been playing professional gardener. Hattie Goodacre, who found herself short-handed in April, asked me to come work for her part time, only 15 to 20 hours a week, and I jumped at the chance. I knew all about the gardening part, back-breaking labor mixed with equal parts bliss, and figured the experience wouldn't be too far from that. Getting out of the house, a break from domesticity, was a plus, as was having a "real" (read "paying") job. I welcomed the opportunity for camaraderie, outdoor work, and a little extra cash with which to indulge my own home and garden.

April 18th

Hattie picks me up on the first day in her small truck. The back of it's covered with ecologically-minded bumper stickers and hippie words-of-wisdom, like "Who

Owns You?" and "Subvert the Dominant Paradigm," "Dare to Legalize Drugs," and "Trees are the Answer." Hattie's ten years older than I, in her 40's, and I'm one of her greatest admirers. She's an individual in a city that's seemingly run by fundamentalist Christians and developers; where marching to the tune of your own drummer is nearly as frowned upon as same-sex marriages. She's an early Hippie and she looks the part, with nearly waist-length, beginning-to-grey hair braided in a ponytail and covered with a floppy straw hat, tie-dye tank shirt, Teva sandals, and dangling jewelry of silver and wood.

We met a few years earlier at the Cooperative Extension's Master Gardener program. I was a student, she was an instructor. I discovered Hattie possessed something rare and precious: a philosophy relating to gardening and her connection to nature. More importantly, she walked the talk. She spends much of her free time on environmental awareness, promoting permaculture, helping to save wild spaces, and non-environmental causes, such as helping the poor. Sensing a kindred soul, I gave her a copy of Michael Pollen's book *Second Nature* while I was taking the master gardening course. She, in turn, invited me to join her garden club. I learned she was also a writer; we became friends.

On our first day working together, we head to the nursery to pick up Feathermeal, a deer repellent. She banters with the help as I take it all in, happy to be part of a new adventure. I'm wearing faded jeans, a green T-shirt, sneakers. I hate hats and have left mine in the truck.

As we pull out of the driveway, Hattie spies the seashell-shaped top of a birdbath, lying near a fence. It's chipped on one side. "Look at that."

"Oooh, garden art."

"I'm going to go ask them what they're going to do with it."

I wait in the truck. It's a throwaway and Hattie claims it. Back in the cab she says, "Bitchin'."

Hattie's also a foster mom for plants. Her home garden's filled with orphans rescued from trash and compost piles.

At the first client's home I meet Hattie's new business partner, a twenty-two year old woman named Jill. Hattie filled me in on the way—Jill's a former class valedictorian, taking some time off from college, she's just bought her own home, a small ranch style house. Hattie discovered her last year, working for $8 an hour for another gardener. When that gardener moved out of state, Hattie snagged Jill. "I could not believe how much she knew," Hattie told me earlier in the truck. "She's a genius." Although Jill knows a lot, she hasn't yet been accepted into the Master Gardener program.

Jill looks younger than I imagined; her short blond hair is pulled into a ponytail, kinda Gidget-y. She wears a big smile and no makeup.

"Man, the nepeta's seeded everywhere," she says when we arrive, "also the asters. We'll need to work on that today. There's also tons of ash tree seedlings."

"Ah, the asters." Hattie winks at me. "I call 'em pain-in-the-asters."

I find that while Jill delights in letting plant-Latin roll effortlessly off her tongue she also speaks Slang-lish; she says "bitchin'" a lot, like Hattie, but her favorite expression is "killer," as in "those were some killer pachysandra."

It's clear Jill and Hattie are tight. They both wear Teva sandals, and carry matching Hori Hori knives Jill ordered through *Horticulture* magazine, in their matching ladies' size leather tool belts. I can't help but be a little envious of their relationship.

The client's home is palatial, with a huge, water-sucking front and back lawns of green, lush Kentucky bluegrass, something I find disgusting in our time of drought. Flowers and shrubs border the lawn on all sides, and a tree-filled wild area sits at the back of the property. Hattie says she's found bear poop out there before and, last spring, a swarm of bees clinging to a tree branch. She also says it's a good place to squat and pee if you have an emergency, since we won't be using the facilities at the house.

I ponder that for a millisecond. I don't think so. While I'm not fearful of wildlife, I don't want to be spied pissing in someone's backyard.

We spend four hours weeding.

The end of the morning finds us on top of a stuccoed cement wall, pulling up ash tree seedlings.

"Damn, this bra is killing me," says Hattie, tugging at the bottom of hers. "Women shouldn't be trussed up like turkeys."

When I get home I feel good, but tired. Spending most of the day out in the fresh air is wonderful.

April 20

This morning I work for another gardener. Kate is Hattie's friend and a brilliant garden designer. She asked Hattie if she could spare someone and Hattie asked if I was interested. I know Kate and I like her; I said sure.

We labor hard at a beautiful hotel, beginning with planting five gallon shrubs all morning long.

The second task is climbing to the top of a fifteen-foot ladder leaning on a stone wall, with five-gallon buckets of soil that probably weigh about thirty pounds. We dump the soil at the top. Heights-neurotic that I am, I'm terrified at the prospect of doing this; luckily one of the younger workers, a British girl, doesn't mind standing on the ladder while we bring the buckets to her. The fair-haired Brit has a nasty sunburn by the time we leave.

At the end of the day Kate tells me that she'll pay me the fifteen dollars per hour, the wage Hattie gives me, but only for today. She says she'd love for me to work for her again but, in the future, can only offer $12. She tells me the other women working for her, including one who is over 40 and has to drive sixty miles round trip to work each day, receive only $10 an hour for this phys-ically-demanding/no benefits/no healthcare work. With no hard feelings, I realize that to her, I'm just a glorified hole digger and bucket hauler. The saddest part of it is $12 is not a bad wage, in this city, at this time, for this type of work. But it's a survival-only wage. My husband is also a contractor, heating and air conditioning, and this is a big reason we've never hired anyone; it would be almost impossible to pay them what we felt was right and we couldn't offer benefits (vacation pay, sick pay, health insurance, etc.) that we ourselves did not enjoy. I'm subcontracting out my labor as a gardener, and it's just not going to be worth it to work for Kate again.

April 22

Today I work with the whole crew, comprised of Hattie, Jill, and two younger women who also work part time, usually on the days I'm off. We crawl over a high, rounded garden bed near a driveway, fill in the few bare spots with new perennials. I've only been a professional gardener for a couple of weeks and I'm still self-conscious. I'm regularly asking Hattie how she does things, what's her technique.

The plants we put in today are bigger than usual, quart size, and we move the thick mulch and dig the holes. There's always a significant mound of soil next to the newly planted addition, in a little pile beside the mulch.

"What should I do with all the extra soil?" I ask. I realize it's a stupid question, but can't help myself, everything is so meticulously groomed.

Hattie laughs out loud. "I'm going to give you an Indian name, 'Extra Soil.' Just smooth it around." I'm grateful she doesn't comment on how uptight I am.

Later she tells me how happy she is I'm working for her. She compliments everyone on a daily basis. It's the first time I've experienced this behavior in a "boss," a word Hattie hates. She refers to all of us as gardening goddesses.

April 24

Hattie doesn't usually pick me up until 9:00, at the earliest, and we don't get to the first garden till after 9:30. I hate getting to the job so late. It feels like I'm not getting enough done at home in the morning, and then, by the time I get home again in the afternoon, I'm worn out. I'd prefer to go out early in the morning, when it's cooler, but Hattie says the clients don't like us to arrive until after 9 A. M. La dee da, I think, who cares if the gardeners have to work in more uncomfortable, hotter conditions?

Hattie and I dig a new bed together at a home I hadn't worked at before, a house they call the "Pink House" because the owner has a preference for pink flowers.

I ask her about rabbit hutches. My husband's building one for our daughters' new rabbit, Oscar, and I'm wondering about hutch size. Hattie's kept rabbits for years. She rhapsodizes about bunny manure; it's the best, it's low in nitrogen so can be put right in the garden and won't burn plants.

"He should make it big," she says of the hutch, while popping out a dandelion.

"It is." I rip out a bindweed vine.

"Real big." She grins wickedly. "A big ass hutch."

I laugh and echo her, "Yeah, a big ass hutch." We snicker together under our straw hats, Heh heh heh, sounding like the female horticultural versions of Beavis and Butthead.

I bought one of the leather tool belts, trying to fit in with Hattie and Jill, I suspect, but I don't like it. Every time I crouch down, a tool pokes or juts out at me. And, as a person who won't leave home without at least some makeup on, it feels a little butch. I've gone back to carrying my tools in a bucket and leaving them, now and then, scattered like rose petals on the job site.

May 10

Today I'm edging a huge flower bed, going along with a shovel, slicing out pieces of sod that are creeping in too close, shaking out the grass from the soil, making a pile of *Pennisetum* for the compost pile. The owner doesn't like the black plastic lawn edging so it's all done manually. Hattie reminds me to switch legs periodically, telling me she blew out one of her knees with the shovel work.

I'm enjoying the gardening, but I can honestly say I'm not too impressed with the neighborhood. While I admire much of the architecture and all of the beauty, it all seems too big, much too big, for so few people. I had a brief experience with poverty as a child. After my mom and dad divorced, my twenty-something mom, me (then seven years old), and three younger siblings lived on welfare for a few years. We drank reconstituted powdered milk, ate "govm't" cheese and canned chicken. Once we received Christmas presents through a charity, including (this was the early 1970s), a used stuffed animal, a donkey. The donkey was adorable but I remember being repulsed. Spending a winter using an outhouse and sharing heated bathwater in a big metal tub by a fireplace is something that only sounds romantic. And you never forget. Seeing all this entitlement and grandiose living feels like a cockle-burr, snagged on the hem of my worn out jeans, prickling me now and again.

May 12

I'm planting annuals, salvia, petunias, lobelia, and dusty miller, in a long built-in planter at the top of a ten-foot-high brick wall on the side of a long driveway. It can only be reached by ladder. My fear of heights is kicked in again and I'm a little shaky but going about my business. I see a bee fly into a small hole in a brick below me. She leaves, then returns, and this time I move down to get a closer look. The bee's carrying a perfectly round piece of leaf. I keep tabs on her and she comes out again, and flies away.

By the time she returns I'm very close, my face about a foot away from the hole's entrance. I'm not worried about being stung as I know she's working, and not concerned with me. As she positions herself for a landing, I get a micro-view. She's holding the leaf with her thin, long for a bee, legs. The leafy green rug's partially rolled up, so it'll fit in the hole. I watch her as she hovers for a few more moments, wings beating rapidly. She's about the same size as a honeybee, stout, hairy, and has a metallic blue cast. She completely ignores me, so intent is she on her work. It's like a TV nature show, a micro-view of one infinitesimal part of nature, but a million times better. It's the coolest thing I've witnessed in a garden yet.

Hattie tells me later I've seen a leafcutter bee. They cut precise circles and ovals out of leaves for their long, tunnel-like nests. The ovals line the bottom and sides. They lay one egg per cell, provision each with a mixture of nectar and pollen, and cap each cell with a circle of green.

"When you see rose leaves with these perfect holes in them, it's the leafcutter," Hattie says. "They cause some damage, but not enough to get worked up about. What's really cool about it all, is that the first egg they lay, the oldest one in the far back of the tunnel, is the last to come out."

I admire the leafcutter for her industriousness. Later I look it up on the Internet and find out the leafcutter, of the *Megachile* species, are natives. They're important pollinators, not aggressive, have a mild sting (milder than honeybees and wasps) that's only a threat when they are handled. Our Colorado entomological expert, Whitney Cranshaw, writes: "Leafcutter bees are solitary bees, meaning that they don't produce colonies . . . Instead, individual female leafcutter bees do all the work of rearing."

May 13

We're on the east side of town, in an upper middle-class neighborhood. The house next door to our client's is a tacky Southern cliché on "having arrived": blindingly white fluted columns (I'm guessing metal) on a Georgian-style brick house sitting in front of an endless void of Kentucky green front lawn studded with white urns, fake flowers, and a Rococo, waterless fountain. All

that's missing is a big pink Cadillac.

Hattie refers to the client next door, where we'll be working, by her first name, Annie. Annie's a gynecologist. In the back garden is a patio and small lawn, the running ground for two amiable terriers, and a koi pond,

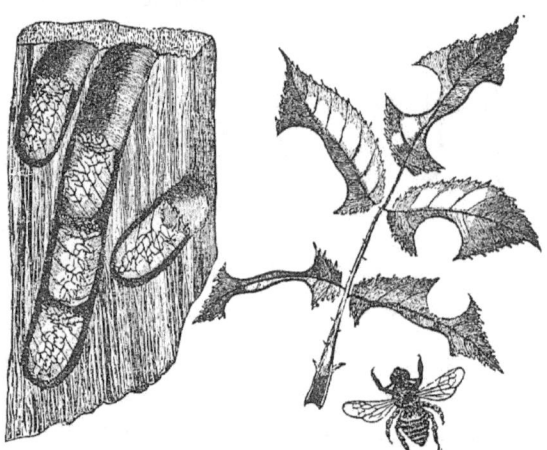

A leaf-cutter bee, its nest, and rose leaves cut by the bee

covered with netting to protect the prize fishes from the occasional hungry blue heron. A huge rock garden surrounds it all. It's built into the surrounding hill, a terraced stone wall topped by an upper garden of boulders and flowers and backed by a parched meadow, a perfect habitat for rattlesnakes.

The day is warm for this time of year, in the upper 80's. We've been drinking a lot of water and I'm thankful Annie has welcomed us to use her bathroom facilities, so we won't have to go at the nearby 7-Eleven. This is a different neighborhood, though; in the Broadmoor we always have to go to the convenience store.

I'm thinking of calling this the Hades garden. On top of the rock wall it's hot and dry, and our weeding, started in different areas, has over the last two hours eventually brought us together. We squat at the top of the property, among the delphinium, yucca, lupine, and soon-to-be scorching stones. I'm the first to finish and when I stand up my head swims. "Whoa, I just got a head rush."

Hattie and Jill find this amusing.

"She just got a twirly," says Jill.

"Congratulations," says Hattie. "Having a twirly is one of the milestones in becoming a gardener."

After some shrub pruning, we gather our tools to leave. Hattie points out a red-tailed hawk soaring above us in the cloudless sky, and I wonder if they're a threat to the koi.

May 15

One of a hired gardener's perks is being able to keep anything they have to weed out. I always defer to Hattie and Jill, but have still scored some coreopsis, pain-in-the-aster, *Knautia macedonica* (red pincushion flower; Hattie calls them "naughty-uh" because of their fecundity), hollyhocks, and even a tiny tree, an *Arborvitae* Hattie potted up personally and presented to me like a gift.

It makes me feel Robin Hoody; taking from the rich. Hattie nurtures orphans in her own garden, gives them to garden club members and to the church where we hold our monthly garden club meetings. Most of the time, though, she relocates them to another of her clients' gardens as freebies. I'm astonished at her non-capitalistic commune with nature through gardening and don't think I'd be so generous.

May 18

We meet at the greenhouse with the garden club members. Hattie's multi-tasking, picking out annuals for both our club's plant sale and for her clients. I'm thrilled because I'm indulging in my all time favorite gardening task, shopping. I buy several flats at wholesale prices, an orgy of annuals.

Hattie and Jill buy a truckload for their clients. Jill raves over some parti-colored striped petunias, hot pink and white, white and dark purple. I think they look circus-like, but keep my opinion to myself.

Later in the day, one of Hattie's favorite clients, a nice sixty-something woman who lives in a Spanish-colonial style townhouse near the Garden of the Gods, goes ga-ga over the petunias Jill picked out.

May 19

We spend a good part of the day at an out-of-town nursery that specializes in herbs. I'm in plant lust mode again, buying herbs and perennials at $1 each for a 2 ½" pot. There are seven different types of basil—Thai, Siam Queen, African Blue, globe, purple leafed, lemon, Genovese; five types of scented geraniums, and oh, so much more!

Hattie wears short shorts and a tank top, her hair up in a ponytail. She's trying to even out, as she calls it, her "gardener's tan," a white-torsoed tan similar to the farmer's version. Hattie's legs are gorgeous but her impressive breasts, I'm guessing "DD," are slightly more on the side of Venus of Willendorf than Venus de Milo.

Hattie doesn't give a damn. I admire Hattie's uninhibited, I-am-beautiful attitude, one that I can only achieve when under the influence of a significant amount of alcohol. Hattie declares herself a primitive, and once told me she would love to live an aboriginal life.

This evening Hattie calls to get my hours—she also pays on time. We bitch about the sprawl in Colorado Springs and she comments about the developers who run our city, "That's their job. Sucking up beautiful places and spitting out shit."

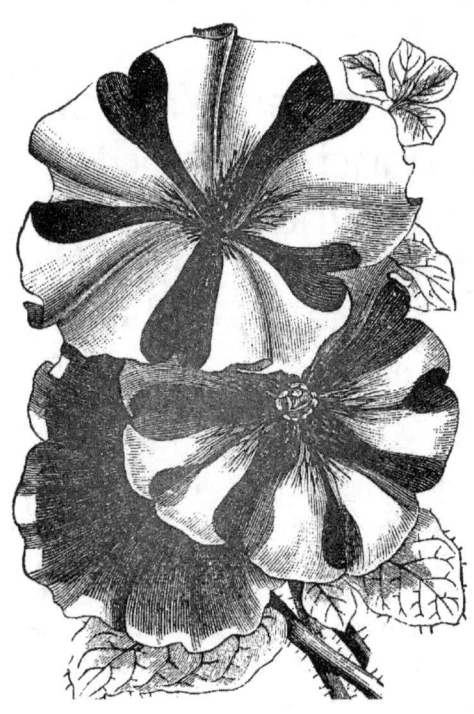

May 20

Hattie seems to genuinely adore most of her clients. This morning we weed and plant 'Lemon gem' marigolds at an elderly man's modest ranch-style house. The home seems to be suburban-boring until I see a contemporary bronze fountain in the back pond. Hattie calls him "sweetie." One of many.

I notice a fledgling robin hopping around the yard, crying to its mother, who delivers food to him. "He'll be fine," says Hattie, "unless a cat comes by."

In the afternoon we're met by the whole crew, plus two more, an older man and woman Hattie hired specifically for the occasion, to plant a truckload of gallon-sized stop-sign colored geraniums in the front of a huge home in a gated community.

We tour the conifer garden, which is expansive and sculptural with only a few flowers. Hattie calls the owner by her first name, Madeline. Madeline is whip-thin, and her pretty, somewhat waxy features remind me of a well-preserved orchid, a prom-queen from ages past. Hattie's sure she's had plastic surgery. Madeline's not a gardener, she's a designer, which means she does all the shopping and directing of where-to-put-what. Hattie tells me of some expensive cast-offs she's received from her, purchases Madeline decided she "didn't quite like" once she got home.

> "Reflexively, I reach down and pull it out. The owner stops, turns to face me. He's angry. 'Why did you do that?' "

This is the first garden I've visited, aside from the hotel's, that bespoke major design savvy. Madeline's garden is Oriental-influence-done-right. Every tree, shrub, and flower is carefully placed, meticulously groomed, and pampered. It's the antithesis of how Hattie and I roll; we tend toward the "wild and wooly" as Hattie calls it. I prefer to think of it as gardening with Nature and letting Nature keep the upper hand.

We begin planting the geraniums and it isn't long before I notice that Madeline's holding an animated conversation with Hattie.

Madeline goes inside and Hattie walks over. She's holding a plastic jar of Osmocote, the time-release fertilizer that comes in tiny beige balls, and some measuring spoons. "Have you guys been putting Osmocote in the planting holes?"

Cindy and I shake our heads. "I didn't know we were supposed to," I say.

"Well, that's what Madeline wants. We're going to have to take them all out and put a rounded teaspoonful in each hole."

"Geez," I say, "what is she, the Osmocote heiress?"

"No," say Hattie. She names a famous electronics company and tells me Madeline's the heiress of that.

May 22

We go to Mike's today for the first time. Mike's a she, the sixty-something widow of a military officer. She's kind of brusque, but I like her. I'm in love with her garden. It's on a hillside, has incredible diversity, and is xeric. I see a lot of plants that I haven't seen in other gardens and covet a bronze Buddha nestled among poppies. Mike's middle-aged son lives with her, as do two small, barking terriers. Hattie leaves Cindy and me there and we weed for three hours.

My friend Susan calls me that evening and asks if I'd like to do a gardening job for a friend of hers, an elderly lady who lives downtown. She has a Spanish colonial-style house, with a built-in planter running down the entire length that needs to be filled with annuals. Susan usually does it for her but she's too busy this year. Would I call her?

I do; and make a date for my very first contract work!

May 23

This morning we're spreading mulch. I get to the job at 9:30 A.M. and have to wait for Hattie and crew for twenty more minutes. I'm irritated, thinking about how I could be home, working in my own garden instead of sitting here not getting paid. It's supposed to be another 90-degree day. When Cindy, another of Hattie's gardeners, pulls up, the owner, a thin, 40ish man comes out and greets us.

He leads us up the long driveway to the house. On the way, I spy a small weed tree sapling, a Siberian elm, notorious in these parts, among the border of shrubs and trees leading up the driveway. Reflexively, I reach down and pull it out.

The owner stops, turns to face me. He's angry. "Why did you do that?"

"It was a weed tree."

His manner is icy and he speaks slowly, as if instructing a child, "I would appreciate it if you didn't remove anything without my permission."

I seethe in silence, thinking, here I am, a master gardener with a B.A., getting chewed out by a homeowner for plucking out a goddamn weed.

It doesn't get any better. The truck 'o mulch arrives as does Hattie, Jill, and another woman whom I've never met—just as it starts getting nice and toasty. We have three wheelbarrows. The assembly line begins. We take turns standing on the truckload of mulch, pitchforking the barrows full, and pushing them up the long, steep driveway, around to the back of the house, through the trees, to dump and spread among a stand of white pines.

Back and up, back and up, over and over. It takes us two hours at a fast clip and I don't know how many trips. It's fun in a way because we kind of get into this competitive thing, where we're hustling, passing each other like we're in a relay, grinning. "Hey, look at me, top this."

I keep asking Cindy if she's okay; she's so red-faced she looks like she's going to pass out, but Hattie says mine is the same. "Are you Irish?" she asks Cindy. Cindy doesn't understand at first and thinks it may be a put-down, about liking to drink or something, but then Hattie says it's a Celtic trait—to get so obviously flushed when exerted. She's of Celtic origin too. This may help to explain our shared pagan leanings.

Meanwhile, The Marquis de Sod, Supreme Protector of Weed Trees, is standing in the shade, watching four attractive, dressed-for-summer women haul wheelbarrow loads up and down his driveway, nearly collapsing from heat exhaustion. I sense he's enjoying himself immensely.

May 24

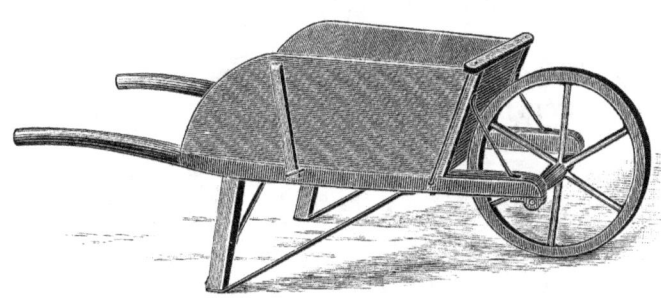

The job for the lady downtown worked out perfectly. I spent Saturday morning buying plants and soil amendment, and I finished it all in one afternoon. It was fun and I made a nice profit. It is so much better being the boss, no matter how perfect your boss may be.

We work in another big money garden today. There's extensive construction going on with the house, adding a new wing to the thousands of square footage already in existence. More weeding, planting of annuals.

As Hattie and I drive homeward, we debate the relative differences of garden tours in her artsy-fartsy, celebrating-diversity neighborhood, where the gardeners are the sole workers and designers, and those in this neighborhood. Our garden club's tour is coming up and we're featuring gardens tended by the club's professional gardeners. Most of the gardens will be in this exclusive section of town.

"The difference," Hattie says, "is that here you get to see what shitloads of money can do for a garden."

"Maybe we should call it the 'Shitloads of Money' tour."

Hattie says that if we had a serious job we'd probably get into trouble together.

May 31

It's another hot day. The year 2000 has been the hottest May in the city's recorded history, and it looks like June will be a scorcher too. Hattie says global warming is undeniable, those who work close to nature have been seeing changes for years. I get up early to water some plants in my own garden and to let the chickens out while everything's dewey and cool, and inside the family's still sleeping. As I walk by a trellis, I see a bee's been slumbering in a poppy and is now crawling out, damp and dew covered. I've heard that if bees are gathering nectar and pollen and it gets too late to return to the hive they'll sleep in a flower. She's unable to fly away until she's dry. I feel blessed to witness this.

I work the morning alone in one of the gardens. Hattie's sent me over to remove a big patch of 'King Alfred' daffodils. She wants to save the bulbs and I'm to put them in trash bags for her.

The 'King Alfreds' are deeply embedded in eighteen inches of muck. I can't believe they are down so deep and that it is so frigging wet. Every time I put the shovel in to pry them out there is a tremendous sucking sound and the gigantic mound resists me, like they're stuck in glue. It takes me over an hour to do a 5 x 8 foot patch, I'm soon wearing platform-mud heels, and I'm cursing under my breath. The water these places use, in a drought, is incredible, it is a bog! When I tell Hattie about the experience, with the instruction "Don't ever send me on a job like that again," she finds it hilarious.

The afternoon is spent at the Hades garden, where at one point, Hattie accidentally breaks off a daylily bud.

"Darn," she says. Then she eats it and says, "yum." I notice she's wearing her wooden, dangling, peace-sign earrings.

(Continued on Page 54)

On Yucca Moths and Four-Leaf Clovers
by
Lucy Bell

Zoe Poster Tilley

The creamy blossom beckoned that early Sunday morning and when I opened the petals, I saw her. My first yucca moth! Nestled near a pollen-heavy stamen, she shifted her position as the sun flooded her hideaway.

My job as a volunteer naturalist at Cheyenne Mountain State Park had immersed me in the amazing world of plants. None fascinated me more than *Yucca glauca*, the native member of the agave family, whose stalks of white flowers rising from a cluster of Spanish bayonet leaves, decorate the fields and hills of Colorado Springs from May to July.

The yucca and the yucca moth represent mutualism, the form of symbiosis in which each species benefits from the relationship. In fact, these two would die without each other.

The yucca moth flies at night, and the petals of the flower spread open in welcome. She collects pollen from the stamens, kneads it into a ball, tucks it under her chin and flies to another yucca plant, where she stuffs it into the pistil, the female part of the flower.

From each grain of pollen a microscopic tube carries the sperm cell down to fertilize the ovules. Before she leaves, she pierces the base of the pistil with her ovipositor and lays three to five eggs. The seeds and the eggs of the yucca moth develop simultaneously. By the time the larva hatch from the eggs, the seeds have developed enough for the larva to eat them. The yucca moth is the only insect that can pollinate the yucca. Yucca seeds are the only food yucca larva can eat.

This story gave me goose bumps, and I wanted to see it for myself. I toyed with the idea of going out in the night with a flashlight to search for the moths, but the closest field was far from my house and remote. I had no desire to meet up with nocturnal predators.

I learned after my discovery that Sunday morning that I didn't need to brave the dark. The yucca flower is the moth's daytime flat, where she rests in preparation for her nighttime activities. It was also her honeymoon suite, the site of her mating, and will serve as the nursery for the babies.

I took my camera with me on my next excursions and began to photograph my findings. Occasionally, the yucca moth would crawl onto my finger. A few times at the dog park while Mollie, my black Lab, patiently waited, I'd call people over to view the moth I'd found and give them an impromptu lecture on mutualism.

My enthusiasm soon had my park colleagues opening blossoms, but at our monthly volunteer meetings they voiced disappointment and a touch of resentment.

"I never find any moths."

"Not even one."

"Lucy, you're just lucky."

"We're giving you a new name—Yucca Momma."

Later that summer I was asked to do a presentation for our meeting. They titled it "Yucca Momma Tells All."

Three years later, I'm still opening yucca blossoms and taking pictures of my little winged friend. I wonder why I am so lucky at this. Is it about intention? Is it about desire?

Several years ago, I was with a group of women at a retreat at Benet Pines Monastery. We'd come inside from a walk and as we sat around the dining room table, Ruth, one of the group, showed us a four-leaf clover she'd found while on the walk.

Everyone was amazed. Only one or two of the seven other women had ever found one, though all of us had looked at one time or another since our childhood.

"Really, you've never found one?" Ruth asked. "Would you like to have one?"

"Oh, yes!" everyone answered, as Ruth left the table and went out the door. In a few minutes she was back with seven four-leaf clovers that she passed out to each of us. Some were smaller than others. Some had a less than perfect leaf edge, but they were indeed all clovers with four leaves.

"How did you do that?" we asked Ruth.

She smiled and shrugged her shoulders. "I wanted to find them, and I did."

Years later, my husband and I were on a road trip and stopped at Chincoteague, Virginia, to get an oil change for our Nissan Xterra. The service station provided a picnic table in a shady area for customers to wait.

Our conversation drifted from topic to topic and something reminded me of the time Vera found the four-leaf clovers. I told the story to my husband, then looking down, I saw clovers growing in the grass beneath our feet. In just a few seconds, I found two four-leaf clovers. They were the first I'd ever found in my life, (and the last).

Mystics and scientists say that we are all part of the same energy. Maybe every now and then we get a hint of that truth. For an instant we are in cahoots with the universe.

The veil lifts and we are one with clovers and moths. ❀

Yucca Mama and Yucca Moth Make Contact by Lucy Bell

(Continued from Page 51)

Before we leave, Hattie dusts everything, not with fairy-dust, but with Feathermeal, the deer-keep-away product. I have never smelled anything so god-awful in my life—it's worse than shit, it's worse than skunk, it's worse than fish emulsion; it's like the ground up, rotting entrails of the most vile sea/land/air creatures imaginable. I can't see how she bears it.

Hattie says it's made out of "chicken parts."

On the way home she stops at a 7-Eleven to wash up and asks me if I need anything. When she comes back to the truck she's got a paper container holding a corn dog, dripping in nacho cheese sauce product. "Sorry," she says, "but I was starving." I'm amazed at Hattie's penchant for junk food.

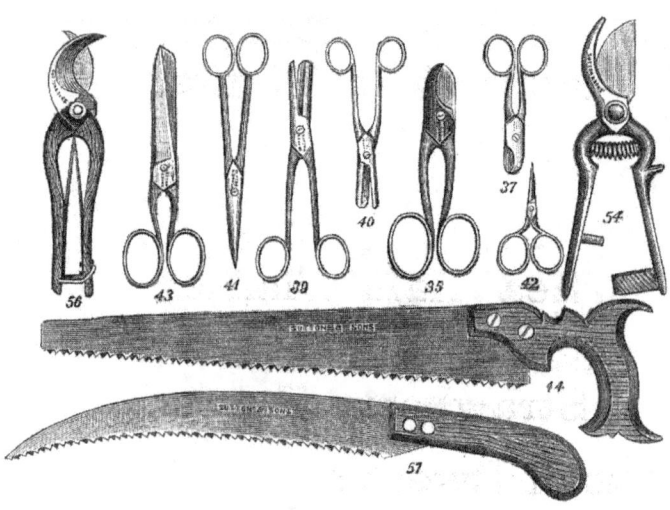

June 4

Hattie sends me to Mike's alone today. As Mike shows me where to work, I comment on a *Salvia argentea*, a huge, hairy-leafed, silver plant now at its rosette stage. Mike says, "Oh, Monty bought that." She says it in a dismissive way that bothers me, the same tone she used when I commented on some interesting pavers that Monty bought. I think it's cool her son's into gardening, and feel sort of sorry for him, that his mom's so prickly.

I weed for a couple of hours in the 90-plus degree heat, then take a thirty-minute lunch break for an iced cappuccino. I'm filthy when I walk in the coffee shop, covered in dirt and sweat, but I feel good, fully endor-phin-ized by the sun and work.

Mike offers some orange hawkweed I'm digging out of her beds, and some other weed, I think it's a malva. "The only name I know it by is "devil's paintbrush," she says of the hawkweed. "I brought it from back East, where it grows wild all over the place. They say it's a terrible weed, but it's so easy to pull up that I don't think it's bad at all." The plant has a low, mounded, hairy-leafed base with thin ten-inch stems that shoot up and are topped by a burnt orange flower cluster. It's sculptural, interesting. Mike's like the flower's base, short, stocky, with short hair. She's interesting too, but, like the weed, not easy to interpret.

She comes out to tell me when it's time to leave, and seems concerned when I don't pack up right away. I finish the area I'm working in, about ten more minutes, and I don't mark it on my card, figuring it would be a nice way to show my gratitude for the pass-alongs. It's been a lonely morning, in a stranger's garden, but I'm excited about the free weeds.

My daughters, Zora, age nine, and Lily, six, have been out of school for almost a week. They hardly miss me at all. They're having a grand time hanging out with Dad, and he with them. The house is about at the same stage of decay as it usually is, so I can't claim things are going to hell.

Years ago, when we were first married, Andy stayed home for a year working on our first home, a Victorian-era house so dilapidated my mom said she wept after her first visit. I know Andy'd like to have the freedom I've enjoyed for the last decade, working at home. I'm surprised at my own feelings of antsy-ness and how I miss them all, like they're having a party that I am not invited to.

June 8

The crew spends the morning at the name-brand heir-ess' home. I hear her and Hattie argue twice. The first time is over some perennials Madeline bought mail order from an expensive East Coast nursery.

They're standing over the tiny plants that Hattie and Jill planted two weeks ago and Madeline says, "I don't understand why they're not doing better."

"Madeline, they're fine," says Hattie. "They've only been in two weeks. They have to establish their root system in the new soil before they'll start having top growth."

This does not please the heiress. "They're just so small. I'm not happy with them."

"You could have bought bigger plants locally, for less money," says Hattie. I cringe. It's Hattie's buy-local-think-global policy; she's not able to resist. "And they would have been acclimated too."

Madeline tosses her well-coiffed head. "I suppose."

Later, when it's almost time to leave, Hattie introduces me to Madeline, telling her I'm "a Master Gardener." This pleases Madeline and she smiles graciously, as do I. I return the Osmocote to the potting shed and run to the back to look for my bypass pruners. Two minutes later I'm back, and find the ladies still standing in the driveway.

"I buy them small, because when you buy a smaller plant, you're going to have a healthier plant," I hear Hattie explain. I notice the object of the conversation is the gallon-sized plant she's holding in one hand, a foot-tall lavender-bloomed clematis that was planted earlier in the trellised area near the driveway.

"I would just like a bigger one," says Madeline.

"It won't take that long for it to grow once it becomes established," Hattie insists. "I guarantee you it will catch up." She smiles at Madeline and I see she's decided to turn on her considerable charm. "Now, what would you rather have, a healthier plant or instant gratification?"

The pause is not as long as a gnat's ass. "Instant gratification," Madeline says. She smiles back at Hattie when she says it, then looks over at me, and I feel a certain naughty (and guilty) admiration for her. Hattie looks dejected.

In the truck, a seething Hattie tells me that Madeline is having all the perennials she special-ordered from some "Fancy East Coast Flower Farm" pulled out.

Later I see that Zora and Lily had a great time with their dad today, as if I haven't spent the last decade of my life being their personal entertainment center and doting, loving, 24/7 momma. I even read them all the Harry Potter books—out loud. What gratitude. Andy's dinner was very good, too.

June 10

Jill and I get into a disagreement over a plant identification at one of her gardens. She's been bounding around happily for the last two hours, fine-tuning whilst I weed, like she's in a personal paradise she created with one hand tied behind her back. I'm jealous; she's younger, in charge, doesn't have children to pine for. She says a plant is fernleaf yarrow, I say it's tansy. The plant isn't in bloom. I remark on the pungent foliage, and smartly share my knowledge that the word tansy comes from the French word for "nose-twister." I have one in my yard.

"It's a fernleaf yarrow!" Jill's exasperated, and I feel oddly satisfied that I have irritated her. This is not like me.

I look the plant up that evening. Jill's right, it is fernleaf yarrow. My feelings for Jill are mixed. I like her and I don't. She seems to have all the answers, her compass confidently pointing to a direction of business ownership and independence at such a young age, when I'm rapidly approaching middle age and I can't really tell where the hell it is I'm headed, though I am beginning to worry it may be an entire life of scraping by and not knowing what I should be doing. My darker side sees Jill as a little know-it-all, wet-behind-the-ears smartass. My honest side says I'm the one being a jerk.

June 13

We're at a surgeon's home and it's one of the most beautiful gardens so far. There's a pool in the backyard and bursting, blooming, lovely English cottage style beds all around, designed and planted by the missus, a highly-educated, likeable, down-to-earth woman. She chats with us and I learn she enjoys shopping at Walmart and Home Depot for plants. That stops me. All this and . . . Walmart? She's the opposite of the franchise queen. Hattie and I refuse to shop at Walmart, knowing that low prices for some come at a steep price for others, namely American businesses and Walmart employees.

This garden would be a glorious place to weed indeed except for one thing. There's dog shit everywhere, complements of an Orson Wells-sized retriever who stays in his kennel while we're there. (His imprisonment's due to his excitable nature—if let loose, I'm told we'd all be humped.) There's definitely something amiss about this dog because his urine, which is also everywhere, reeks.

As I weed, gingerly avoiding turds, longing for a tussy-mussy to hold to my nose, I wonder at the mess. While I am far from fastidious, this is beyond even my level of tolerance. I think, surely if these people can afford three gardeners to come out, at twenty dollars an hour apiece, can't they afford to hire someone to pick up the dog shit?

At another garden the tasks include braiding daffodil foliage. The flowers are wilted and gone, the long green leaves of the daffodils are floppy and, I suppose, not pretty enough to display as is, and yet the bulb needs the energy garnered from those green leaves so they cannot be cut off. I feel absolutely ridiculous braiding daffodil foliage. For some reason it reminds me of extravagant pubic hair grooming, like when a relative told me she had her bush trimmed into a heart shape in celebration of Valentine's Day. Just (ugh) too much.

June 15

We're in Hades again, weeding together in a group, Hattie, Jill and I. June is also turning out to be the hottest on record and we're getting bitchy. Hattie asks me what's my astrological sign.

"Capricorn."

"Oh, Capricorn," she says, lifting an eyebrow. "My mom's a Capricorn, I know all about you." Her tone is definitely on the smart-alecky side, with the tiniest hint of hostility, and I wonder what she's getting at. She's mentioned she and her mom have been at odds many times, over religion, politics, life in general.

"Well, what's yours?"

"Libra."

Well, I'll be damned, I think. My mom's a Libra and I can see some similarities between Hattie and Mom, the perhaps just slightly too fun-loving, living-for-the-day attitude, the belief that their world view is the only world view.

"Ha," I say, "I know all about you, too."

June 17

A good day. I catch my first snakes and am stung by a wasp. I know it doesn't sound good, but for me, Mrs. Wild at Heart, it was exciting. Both occur at The Remmick's, a house with another big rock wall garden, two doors down from Hades. I dubbed it Hades II. In the morning, I spot a yellow jacket and tell Jill. Hattie says it's probably nesting in the wall and the owner will spray because yellow jackets are aggressive. To verify this, within two minutes I'm stung, and endure a white-hot sensation on my wrist, but only for a few minutes. I feel rather proud of my ability to endure wasp-venom.

An hour later I notice the snake.

Jill's nearby and I call her attention to it.

"Get it," she says, and, not thinking, I snatch. My gloved hand comes back with two snakes. One about a

foot long and the other a few inches smaller, both brilliant green with yellow stripes. My heart lurches but I don't squeal.

Luckily, Jill has the weed bucket ready and I'm able to drop them in immediately. They slither up the bucket's sides, frantically trying to escape. I squirm.

"Grab some weeds," orders Jill. I gather some up from the drying pile on the lawn and drop them over the snakes. They chill out.

"See, they just want some cover."

"Woo-wee!" says Hattie, who's joined us.

Jill leaves to get a shirt, to tie over the top of the bucket with a bungee cord.

"My God," I say. "I've never even held a snake before. It's a good thing I had gloves on, or I wouldn't have done it."

Hattie chuckles. "Your eyes were pretty big. Jill will take them home, put them in her garden. It's not a good idea to have them here. Annie next door, her boy-friend's killed snakes before."

"Ribbon snakes? Why?"

"Cause she's terrified."

"But they're beneficial."

"Tell that to someone standing on a lawn chair, screaming," says Hattie. "Oh, by the way, sweetie, you've completed the second milestone that certifies you as a true gardener."

I feel a kinship towards Jill. I would have loved to take the snakes home but my chickens would probably have made a meal of them.

June 20

We're back in the Shitloads of Money area and I suspect Jill may have been smoking Mother Nature. She has that goofy, very-pleased-with-it-all look, and she's admiring the bush clematis a little too much.

Suddenly I hear bells playing, "It's a 'Grand Ole' Flag.' "

"Where's that coming from?" I ask Hattie.

"Oh, it's the carillon in the church, up on the hill. It plays each noon."

"Does it always play that song?"

"Sure does," says Hattie. She rolls her eyes.

The extra-happy gardener walks by and says, "Wow, isn't that something?"

"You should of heard it earlier, Jill," I say. "They played 'Ain't Nothin But a Hound Dog.' "

"Really?" she asks.

She is so stoned. I'm practically bubbly too, with a feeling of superiority. I would never arrive at a client's house in such a condition, though I do remember smoking pot with my boss once, at Jill's age, at work. Oh yeah, I also got pretty intoxicated with that same boss during a luncheon celebration on my 21st birthday. Perhaps I should lose the smugness.

June 21

I've been checking out starting my own gardening business during my days off and I found my second job today when I called a city office about getting a business license. The woman I spoke to said, "You're a gardener? I need one." We set an appointment. As with the other job, I don't tell Hattie or Jill.

June 24

I'm at Mike's again, by myself. It is yet another 90-plus-degree-plus day. Maybe I should name this garden Hades III. After doing a lot of weeding her son drops by and says hi. He's a nice, kind of a doughy, middle-aged guy. I think he's in medicine. Mike has me cut down the poppies, telling me I can save the decorative seed heads if I like, then goes into the house. As I'm performing this task near their sliding glass doors I have this creepy feeling that I'm being watched.

The last thing I do is put up a trellis and try to attach the incredible mess that's lying all over the ground that is a honeysuckle vine. I do the best I can, wrestling with the son-of-a-seed, but it ends up looking far from per-

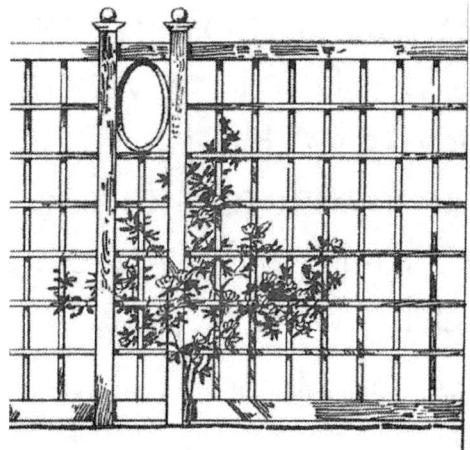

fect. I stay a few minutes longer, but Mike's a nice lady; I don't mind, I want to finish the work. I don't record it.

Hattie calls me that night and says Mike doesn't want me to come over any more; she'd like another gardener. She says I took too long to cut down the poppies. I'm stunned. I've never been fired in my life. I didn't dawdle. I wonder if it irritated her that I liked her son's contributions to the garden, or maybe she thought I was charging her for the extra time I spent there. Maybe she didn't like that I took a 30 minute lunch break or thought I spent too much time admiring her flowers (though I didn't think so). I knew she was hyper-aware of the time clock. I decide I probably wasn't nose-to-the-grindstone enough for her. Or, maybe, I didn't "know my place."

After some smarting and squirming, I realize I can't waste time caring about this. I am still happy about Mike's gift of free plants.

The client/service thing is really getting to me. I've gone nearly a decade free as most can ever hope to be, and am now like a tiger lily stolen from the wild and crammed into a pot. I don't like it. I fear I'm ruined for the work force, I'll never be any good in the rat race. Even though this may signal an inevitable decline down the road, for now the awareness of this is sweet.

June 29

I complete my second freelance gardening job this weekend.

The woman's name on the telephone was Iris, which I took as a good omen, and she lives alone in a newer neighborhood in a modest-sized house. When we meet I see she's about fifty, pretty, quite feminine; her home is tastefully furnished. I admire her rose-patterned antique china in her antique oak hutch. She wants to start a garden, she's sick of the grass, but

"She's young, blonde, skinny with huge boobs, in the biggest SUV money can buy this side of a Hummer. I've come across one of the area's indigenous species, a trophy wife."

doesn't know a thing about the green world. She would like a couple of trellises with vines, and a planter on her front porch with perennials, ditto a small bed in back. I visit her grounds which include a patchy weed filled backyard and two small flower beds with fever-few seedlings and a few snapdragons. She covets her neighbor's garden, an enclosed paradise of honeysuckle vines and roses. We visit it together.

I am unloosed to design this woman's garden and during my ecstatic shopping excursion I buy extra-feminine flowers in multiples: pasque flower, columbine, oriental poppy, salvia, ladies mantle, 'Johnson's Blue' geranium, siberian iris, 'Kent Beauty' oregano, pink baby's breath, 'Husker Red' penstemon, double hollyhocks, daylily, 'Hidcote' lavender and 'Rose Queen' salvia. Several roses: a dark rose and white Meideland for her porch, a 'John Davis' climbing rose for the new bed below her deck, and a 'Fairy' polyantha for a large pot. A few vines: clematis tangutica, Hall's honeysuckle and trumpet creeper 'Madame Galen' will begin the softening of her fenced-in backyard. And of course, I add a few bags of soil amendment. I find a playdate for the girls on Saturday so Andy can help me haul two fan trellises for the fence and two trellis panels to cover and beautify the space below her back deck. He hangs them for me.

I love it.

I can see how I could develop my own business easily. Problem is, while I love creating gardens, I love writing, and being home, so much more. The seed of a green-hearted novel's been germinating and now it's demanding to be cultivated on paper. And it's been almost a month since my girls got out of school. Even part time is too much time away.

July 3

On the day I begin creating childlike scenarios of intrigue with worms, dandelions, and bluegrass and then tiptoe through sexual-in-nature garden fantasies, I take a 12:40 pee break at the Shitloads of Money neighborhood gas station/convenience store. I drive my seven year old Taurus, and as I stop at the intersection right next to the store, a man, about to cross the street on foot, stops too. He waves my car on, his gestures grand. As I pull in the parking lot he walks by and says, "THANK YOU!"

His rudeness unsettles me. Was I supposed to insist he cross before me? Oh, no, sir, after you! As I dig for change in my purse a woman pulls up at the pumps. She's young, blonde, skinny with huge boobs, in the biggest SUV money can buy this side of a Hummer. I've come across one of the area's indigenous species, a trophy wife. She leaves the behemoth running while she darts into the store. Here it's safe to leave a new vehicle running, door unlocked. No car thief would be so incredibly stupid in this part of town, where police service is probably almost instantaneous. I'm angry at the jerk at the crossroad and sorely want to pass it on to the trophy bride, to yell, "Hey, gas waster, turn off your damn engine!"

The community toilet that we gardening ladies share with all the gentlemen workers in the area (pool men, lawn mowing men, tree men, construction workers, a man for every need, nothing too great or small) is half-clogged. I won't go into the disgusting, sickening details. I'm afraid to flush, but I'm near bursting, so I pee anyway, hovering. After I pull up my pants, I push down the handle and move away from the seatless toilet as fast as I can. The contents, thankfully, go down. My bile rises.

Our clients. Would it be too much to offer facilities at their homes, for their hired help who are busting their asses to make their lives more magically beautiful? Really, would an outhouse be too dear? I think how Hattie could make even an outhouse tres chic, covered with vines and roses. It would definitely be better than this communal shithole. Then I wonder why I'm wasting my time thinking about what the privileged should do.

Sheri Armstrong, canstockphoto.com

That afternoon at the Rennick's I share my idea. I've temporarily gotten over my shitty mood because at this house I have some company. I'm not all by myself, going crazy.

"Great idea," Hattie says. "Only problem is, the workers would probably use it as a place to smoke pot."

I hadn't thought of that. So, who cares?

I bitch a little more and Hattie tells me that in all the years she's been a gardener, she's never gotten so much as a card on Christmas from the Shitloads of Money crowd.

July 8

By the second week in July, all the new installations have gone in, the flowerpots and hanging baskets and windowboxes have been filled. The weeds are under control. Now it's just mind-numbing maintenance. Deadheading, endless weeding. I don't want to be a hired gardener any more, and I'm a little doubtful I'll ever start my own gardening business. It's too hard physically, it's too hard on the ego, and I don't like being away from my daughters when they are home all day during the summer. Life's too short. I tell Hattie that

I'm going to leave, that I want to get back to writing and my family. She understands.

I feel liberated.

Postscript: February 12, 2001

I had a physical legacy from the gardening experiment, my right elbow ached for months. Tennis elbow, from using a shovel, doing the manual lawn edging. It finally stopped this week. I can't wait to get back to gardening this year, in my own garden.

I talked to Hattie last night. She said she didn't last the summer with the heiress. The green grind also took its toll on Jill, and she decided in the fall to enroll in nursing school. She's able to make enough through waitressing a few nights a week to pay the bills. Waitressing—another service job, but one that is lucrative compared to creating beauty and toiling in the soil. I'm sorry that things weren't anywhere near as rosy for Jill as I had imagined.

Hattie says she'll start looking for some more crew members in a month or so. She says she thinks gardening must be a calling, as there are many who try it and don't stay with it. Only she's reached those other milestones of the true gardener, ones that may forever remain a mystery to me. ❁

Hooked on Books

Over 250,000 titles

"A book lover's dream come true."

3918 Maizeland Road
(at N. Academy)
Colorado Springs, CO 80909
(719) 596-1621

Used Books and Discounted New Books
hookedonbooks@qwestoffice.net

"Apple Tree in Winter" by Verne Morton.
From *Handbook of Nature Study*, 1947.

Winter Garden

by Jane Knechtel

The black earth brooding.
Cowering roses half-dressed each night.
Daphne begging to be let in.
Flirting primroses—
Bulbs squirming, in labor.
The dogwood stoic. Skeletal.

Red Rock Canyon in January

by

Rhonda Van Pelt

Naked Ladies by Laura Chilson

Sex in the Garden
An Underground Affair
by
Elisabeth Kinsey

Do you remember your first kiss? How about your first lover? Well, during winter, that's what we gardeners must do. We must remember the sweet earth of our gardens, even while it's blanketed and hibernating under ice and snow. I'm living without my husband again, therefore, my sexual relationship is nil. If you'd like to think of me engaging in infidelity, go for it. I'm boringly devoted, though. Ignore that for this column. Let's pretend I'm very naughty and am having an affair with the bulb. Like winter can be for gardeners, traipsing around with the memory of luscious dirt on our hands and longing for that tactile transference between hands and earth, we can envision all the boyfriends (and girlfriends) of our past in full detail. I remember one of my Berlin boyfriends, when I lived there as a nanny, to have a particularly sweet breath when he blew on my ear. Oh my, here we go. I'm planting the memories of every Berlin boyfriend in the ground this fall. What will spring bring me?

What possibly can a currently sexless gal say about sex in the garden at this time of year? My friends tell me—talk about the produce section, sexy vegetables like cucumbers and the longer sweet potatoes. But I'm thinking of a certain tactile tuber, glabrous, yet man-like. And the image of a flowering naked lady. Although these "naked lady" bulbs don't grow in Colorado, in my California childhood I planted them with my grandmother. Grandmothers can be sexy, c'mon. Instead of a MILF, the ones who hold bulbs in their hands loosely, and drop them gently into the crevice of the ground, those are called GILFs.

That particular bulb got its name or its "nakedness" from their bulbous promise, when they jut forward in spring, thrusting up only green spikes, without anything to show; naked, in fact, until at the ends form a bulky bud. When their flower pulses forth, opening into, in this case, an amaryllis, their ruddy pinks aren't bashful as they dance in your front yard.

Which bulbs give you the most wham-bam-thank you-Ma'am for your buck? There are too many to list but some of my faves are the many hybrids of tulips. Plant them anytime; but usually, in Colorado, you'll need to open the earth as it still offers a supple surface, mostly in late September or October. Crocus, hyacinth, and mini-daffodils cluster around the spring, popping color at your feet, as if you are the queen and they cower and lust for your presence. Plant the tiny joys around the tall and papery iris and you'll be sure to excite anyone walking by in spring.

> "Crocus, hyacinth, and mini-daffodils cluster around the spring, popping color at your feet, as if you are the queen and they cower and lust for your presence."

Not all bulbs are bulbs. You can't be fooled by their testi-like appearance. Corms are described as being "swollen, underground" and only have one "growing point." A gladiola and crocus have this base. There are rhizomes which lay on their backs, growing horizontal. Lily of the valley will take over a whole yard, inseminating the air with their heavy scent, but only in milder climates with enough humidity (University of Illinois, 2012). Denver would have to exhale, all at once, an exalted breath after sex, to create that kind of humidity. Tubers mass-propagate the dahlia and begonia, bulbs broad in the middles, pulsating out in bunches under the surface tuft (Dave's Garden, 2012).

What can a gardener do with these tempting underground treasures? There are so many bulbs, and so much lust for the earthen tubers. One bulb enthusiast had a positive experience planting the naked lady, or amaryllis, in Tucson. She wrote, "I'm from Tucson, AZ and my Uncle Charlie brought some bulbs out from Minnesota to me . . . I have planted them on the west side of my home but has afternoon shade from my Southern Oak trees." Joan

Bolten (2012) of Santa Barbara Garden Design claims on her blog: "In August, the show begins, seemingly overnight. Stout, brownish-purplish stems rise rapidly out of the earth." The rising is what sustains our thoughts through winter. In spring, as with all creatures, the libido returns, and our buried jewels thrust up from a cracked, warm earth.

Bulbs are like an orgasm, they will burst forth in folds if you coax them out of the ground. Bulbs promise spring sex, and, during the winter, we can envision scenes of that rampant flowering. Plant

> "In spring, as with all creatures, the libido returns . . ."

them in Fall, and sense their growing interest, as they sustain your enthusiasm through winter. One day you will see flat dirt. The next, a shoot will be unsheathed, and finally, you'll see gold, purple, reds, oranges, and pinks dot and dance, undulating and naked. What would my grandmother think of this carnal scene? Well, she's the one who planted them. I'm sure she remembers all the boyfriends of her past, too. We're all human.

Bibliography
1. Joan Bolten, Santa Barbara Garden Design, http://www.santabarbaragardens.com/articles/128_amaryllis_nls/arti_128.php
2. University of Illinois Extension. 2012
3. Dave's Garden http://davesgarden.com/guides/pf/go/2377/

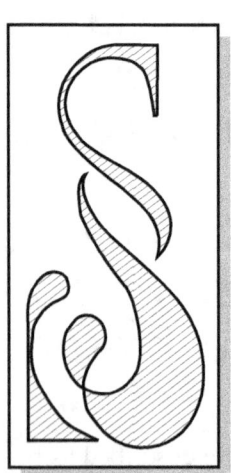

❖ SPIELARTS PUBLICATION DESIGN

❖ SITE-RITE WEB DESIGN

Book / Magazine & Website design
Illustration, Graphic design, Fine art

www.site-rite.net
719.630.7324

www.spielarts.com
paul@spielarts.com

TOOLS AND TALENT TO BRING YOUR VISION INTO REALITY

Fifty Shades
of Green

Edited by
Cheri Colburn

Gardening just got dirtier.

Available at Amazon.com
paperback and Kindle

Conifers

A Vintage Illustration by Joseph E. Ebertz

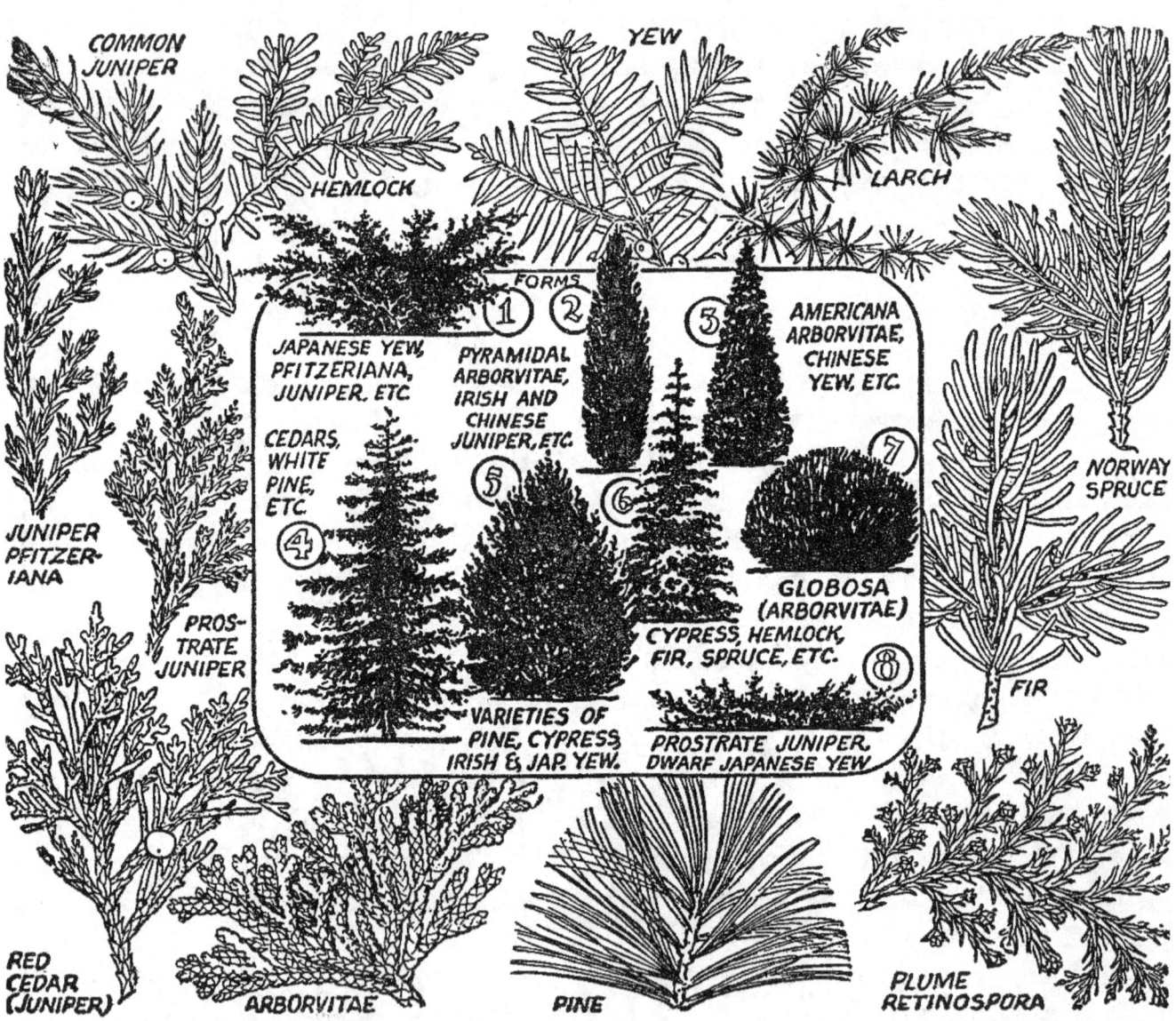

Leafing Through
a review of books, etc.

on organic matter, composting, and microbial inoculants are all important aspects that we should all follow.

I would recommend this book, but with the caveat that you read, compare, and contrast it with other organic gardening books, articles, and scientific research. —*Larry Stebbins*

Building Soils Naturally: Innovative Methods for Organic Gardeners
by Phil Nauta
(Acres USA, 2012)

I was excited to get to read this book. Finally an entire book devoted to organic soil practices and principles. My mother used to say, "There are many ways to make spaghetti sauce but they all start with good tasting tomatoes." It is somewhat similar with soil. There are some simple principles that are universal. Nauta touches on most of them in this comprehensive study.

However, as I was reading, Nauta made some claims that to me seemed outrageous. The traditional scientific body of knowledge and the known laws of physics are not in agreement with such things as biological transmutation (the plant's ability to change one element, like potassium into calcium) or "Light is guided down to the root zone along the roots." In my opinion, he also could have left out the comments on how plants know a storm is coming and "they know how you feel about them." This soft science, if you can call it that, takes away from what could be a landmark book.

Since there is a good deal of both practical and statistical information it makes it difficult to know how well researched his facts are! I do agree that you need a comprehensive soil nutrient test to determine a practical course of remediation for your farm or backyard garden. That being said, very few gardeners will go down that road (farmers maybe). To Nauta's credit, the information

Confessions of an Rx Drug Pusher
by Gwen Olson
(iUniverse, 2009)

We probably all know someone who is undergoing a drug treatment for a psychiatric disorder; whether it is antidepressants, anti-anxiety medication or stimulants for disorders like ADHD. And while *Confessions of an Rx Drug Pusher* is not directly about gardening or the environment, this book is something that everyone who is concerned with living a natural and healthful life should read.

The author spent fifteen years as a sales represenative in the pharmaceutical industry so she knows whereof she speaks. According to her website she has worked for health care giants Johnson & Johnson, Syntex Labs, Bristol-Myers Squibb, Abbott Laboratories, and Forest Laboratories.

The memoir begins with an account of the tragic death of Olson's niece Megan. It was terrible to read about her suicide and the emotional impact of this story was almost debilitating enough to keep me from reading further. However, the cautionary message must be spread; mind-altering drugs can profoundly impact a person's mental state, and this effect is not always the intended treatment. It was both interesting and frightening to learn that using antidepressants, as well as trying to cease using them, can not only increase suicide risks but can facilitate violent behavior in some individuals.

Gwen Olson points out that it is easy to trust the pharmaceutical experts in matters of physical and mental health. That is what they are getting paid for, right? It is vital to know the exact kinds of ethical problems pervading the drug industry today. Olson points out several, including: giving incentives (like extravagant lunches) to doctors who are willing to listen to representatives; seeking out high volume prescribers, or as the big pharmaceutical companies call them, "HVPs;" and being unconcerned with the elimination of disease and disorder, but concerned with constant revenue generated with symptoms, maybe even those that arise from taking the drugs being used to treat another ailment. I also learned from this memoir that in many cases drugs are prescribed to groups that were not represented in clinical trials. For example, drugs being prescribed to children, when the trials conducted on approval for the medications were on adults over eighteen years old.

After this year, I will have received my psychology degree, and while I do know more than the average person about the effects of psychiatric medications, I have never read something that has urged against their use so strongly.

In essence, the memoir breaks down the addictive and debilitating properties of psychoactive drugs, antidepressants in particular.

Gwen Olsen's book is a painfully honest account of her experiences with mental illness in her family, and her career as a pharmaceutical representative. At times, this account is so honest that I found myself cringing, but I am touched by her sincere and noble divulgence to the reader. Since psychiatric drugs have crept into the everyday lives of many Americans, it is important that everyone educate themselves on this subject. While not an enjoyable reading experience, this book is profoundly impactful and leaves the reader with a broader and deeper insight into one of America's most corrupt industries.

—*Zora Knauf*

Grow Cook Eat: A Food Lover's Guide to Vegetable Gardening
Willi Galloway, with photographs by Jim Henkens
(Sasquatch Books, 2012)

All cookbooks and gardening guides should aspire to be like *Grow Cook Eat*, a marvelous hybrid by Willi Galloway. As the title reveals, she begins with food early in its life cycle, at the garden-planning stage, and takes the reader along through production, the kitchen, and to the table.

Chapters include "Gardening Fundamentals," "Greens," "The Cabbage Family," and "Warm-season Vegetables," with extensive information on planting, growing, harvesting, storing, cooking ideas, and delicious varieties. Tips and recipes are interspersed throughout and perfectly complemented by Jim Henkens' mouth-watering photos, some taken in Galloway's own garden.

Galloway lives in Oregon, but not to worry; this book should easily translate to Colorado's climate and altitude. She has lived and loved her subject matter and is down-to-earth about it, acknowledging that most readers will not have the time to make grand gestures with their gardening and cooking:

"Growing a big mix of greens means that putting a healthy meal on the table is never more than 30 minutes away. Bring the basket of a salad spinner—one of the world's best inventions—right out into the garden and fill it with whatever strikes your fancy . . . if cooking just isn't in the cards one evening, add a veneer of wholesomeness to a frozen pizza by tossing big handfuls of arugula on top of it just before it comes out of the oven."

Whether you're a rookie gardener or a callus-handed veteran, you'll probably learn something new about the art and science of gardening, such as storing leftover seeds, benignly controlling pests, or turning your guests "loose in the garden to harvest and create their own custom blend" of herbal tea. If you don't have a garden, you'll at least learn to respect where food comes from.

She even scatters in a bit of history, as when she mentions Dutch gardeners who introduced orange carrots in the 1600s (a few sentences later, she also mentions Bugs Bunny), and turns tour guide with visits to the gardens and markets of Mexico and Cuba.

She knows how important visual pleasure is in the garden and on the table, and she recommends the best combinations of textures and colors, as in this passage about dill: "This versatile herb looks cheerful when planted behind zinnias, short orange cosmos, and annual coreopsis. The flowers disguise the herb's lanky stems and, along with the dill's blossoms, attract parasitic wasps and other pollinators to the garden."

I must admit, Galloway may have cured me of my lifelong distaste for most root vegetables, which she calls "miraculous." I can't wait to try her recipes for oven-roasted beets and cider-glazed baby turnips.

"Most root crops produce tasty tops, flower buds, and even seedpods, in addition to their roots. Learning how to harvest these extra edibles and use them in the kitchen is an easy way to increase the productivity of your garden and extend the harvest season."

Feast on this book and you'll never garden or cook the same way. You'll certainly never eat the same way again.
—*Rhonda Van Pelt*

(P. S. You can check out Galloway's blog at www.digginfood.com for recipes and more informatio. —Ed.)

The New American Landscape: Leading Voices on the Future of Sustainable Gardening
Edited by
Thomas Christopher
(Timber Press, 2011)

The culture of sustainability and environmental responsibility has been gaining steam for several years now. More and more people from all walks of life have been re-evaluating their lifestyles, leading them to change their thinking and actions concerning the way they treat the planet and what they want the future to look like. It's a true groundswell that is arcing towards a real sea change. Good evidence of this shift is the recent emergence of the book, *The New American Landscape: Leading Voices on the Future of Sustainable Gardening.*

Edited by Thomas Christopher, this book compiles eleven essays by professionals, academics, and experts in the field of sustainable gardening and landscaping. The purpose of the book seems to be to document and promote an emerging movement that has people transforming their yards and landscapes into more eco-responsible and resource-friendly spaces.

In these pages you will read about converting conventional lawns from resource-depleting monocultures into lush meadow gardens and healthy natural lawns. John Greenlee, a long-time advocate of meadow gardening, describes how to make this transformation and explains the benefits of doing so.

There is also a discussion by Rick Darke about replacing exotic plants with native plants, including when to consider exotics and why they are not always the wrong choice: "Perhaps our thinking will evolve away from worrying about whether plants are native or not, and toward a valuation of how they function in today's ecology."

Eric Toensmeiser suggests ways to make our edible gardens more sustainable and introduces a concept known as mycoscaping, which includes growing edible mushrooms in the compost and mulch right below and alongside plants in the garden. David W. Wolfe addresses the challenges of gardening in a changing climate and offers ways in which we can change our approach to gardening in order to deal with these challenges. Waterwise gardens, green roofs, wildlife-friendly landscaping, and healthy soil management are also discussed in these pages. While this book is not a comprehensive source for these concepts (some of which are long-standing and others just emerging), the introductions are extremely helpful and stimulating and the suggested resources found throughout the book are invaluable.
—*Daniel Murphy*

On the Future of Food: The Prince's Speech
By HRH The Prince of Wales
Forward by Wendell Berry;
Afterword by Will Allen and
Eric Schlosser
(Rodale, 2012)

At the Future of Food Conference (Georgetown University, May 4, 2011) Prince Charles gave a keynote speech that is now available for all to read. It's no secret that over the years he has championed organic gardening and sustainable food practices. What is refreshing is that the rest of the planet is hearing about it. Of course he is not the only voice, but when royalty speaks we do tend to listen.

As Prince Charles points out, our planet will reach a population of nine billion in just a few decades. The problem is how to feed everyone in a way that is not damaging to our soils, air, and water supplies. The author's passion for all the concerns should be taken very seriously. As food supplies dwindle, political unrest is a certainty. He also points out that the industrial food methods used today may not serve us well in alleviating any such unrest.

This important short pamphlet is a call to action for all of us. Developed nations throw away over 40% of the food that is purchased while developing nations lose 40% of their food between farm and market (due to lack of proper storage and transport). Topsoil is being depleted at an alarming rate and chemical fertilizers are slowly degrading our water systems. We can make a difference by demanding more ecologically sound practices in our food system. His straight talk is sure to inspire many.

I recommend this read for all those that believe that we can feed the world and heal our planet at the same time.

Note: The Prince has his share of detractors. Some are displeased with the lavish way in which he lives. Perhaps it sets a double standard about how everyone but royalty should modify their lifestyles to help save the planet.
—*Larry Stebbins*

Buckley's
HOMESTEAD SUPPLY

- Cheese making supplies

- Soap making supplies

- Yogurt making supplies

- Ranch-way feed for goats, rabbits and chickens

- Canning supplies

- Vintage-looking aprons and kitchen linens

- Locally crafted soaps

- Classes such as Soapmaking, Herbal Remedies and more!

- And much, much more!

(719) 358-8510 • 1501 W. Colorado Ave., Colorado Springs, CO
www.buckleyshomesteadsupply.com

Natural Health 4 Wellness
NaturalHealth4Wellness.com
nh4w.com

Natural Skin Care
Dry skin
Problem skin
Normal & Combination Skin

Natural Hair Care
Dry Hair
Problem Hair
Scalp Issues

We Specialize In:
*natural curls, waves, coils,
naturally straight &
textured tresses*

Health & Wellness
600+ Health & Wellness Products

* Nature's Sunshine Products
* Cleanse & Detox
* Nutritional Supplements
* Herbal Supplements
* Flower Essences (liquid extracts)
* Essential Oils (aromatherapy)
* Natural Weightloss
* Vitamins & Minerals
* Green Superfoods
* Vegan Protein Powder (drinks)
* Body System Packs & more!

Visit Us Online:
FREE Natural Health Classes
FREE Ask Us Service & Assessment

The Juniper

a zine about living the small, slow, simple life

gardening, riding bikes, and doing it yourself

grow it from seed...get there by bike

send a dollar or stamps for the latest issues

Dan Murphy
PO Box 9862
Boise ID 83707
USA

juniperjournal@hotmail.com

www.juniperbug.blogspot.com

Sunfire

A Collection of Poems

James A. Ciletti

Yoga
with
Pat

www.dancingheartsstudio.com

**Also
check out . . .**

**Quilts by Pat
Jewelry by Frank
Pastels by Peggy**

Top Dressing
Gifts That Give by Becky Elder

"Some purchase with plastic, some use savings or what cash they have on hand to pay for 'thoughtfulness' expressed in a present. We all think: 'Gotta get such and such for so and so . . .' "

Gift giving from the heart (not expecting anything in return) is a blessed event, an expression of love, gratitude, and kindness. Yet, often there's an expectation that builds up over the years, as well as a delicate "give-get" balance among family and friends. If there's too much focus on the gift, the heartfelt meaning is drained away and lost.

Many are taking steps toward shopping differently; they are learning to build local economy and sustainability by "voting" with their money. Did you know that shopping at small, privately-owned businesses helps your whole community? Roughly 68% of every dollar spent in a local business stays local and helps that economy thrive. Tim Mitchell in Northwest Earth Institute's Choices for Sustainable Living states, "A dollar spent at a locally owned store is usually spent 6 to 15 times before it leaves the community. From $1, you create $5 to $14 in value within that community."

The personal experience of shopping locally is enhanced by avoiding the malls and canned music; during the holidays, one may even avoid long lines, crabby helpers, traffic jams, and the incessant pressure to buy more. Why not support and even make friends with the business owners in your neighborhood instead? It is pleasant for them too, as their shop is their life, their joy, and their survival . . . almost their home!

To be even greener, we can also consider what we are purchasing. There are many shops full of "made in China" meaningless items. Ask yourself: "Do I really

want to buy something that is plastic? Is this gift healthful? Is it delicious? Is it art? Will it last? Who is supported by my purchase?" If you have doubts, don't buy it.

If you are an expert treasure hunter, you can shop your local thrift stores. Their recycled impact is a positive plus! Truly wonderful handmade gifts can be found at holiday sales, art shows, art shops, farmers' markets, estate and garage sales.

If you're in an inventive spirit, you can create your own gifts of love. In years' past, I have given floral displays from my own garden, live plants with ribbons and little adornments, and books of quotes, photos, and poetry. One year for holiday gifts I made refrigerator magnets for family and friends from old photos. I added "conversation" from the Sunday comics. They are still up on various kitchen appliances—and we still laugh!

I love to put together containers full of goodies—baked goods, handmade soaps, shiny apples, candles, delicious foods from the farmers market, fair trade cacao treats, garden seeds, cool snags from the thrift store, and gift certificates from local stores. Of course, the most meaningful touch is the handwritten letters and cards—there is nothing like expressing your love in your own script and sentiments.

Yeah, we can shop, we will shop. But our holidays and other times of gift-giving are for us, not shopping. Try a local and homespun holiday this year . . . the rewards will surprise you. ✳

www.ingramcontent.com/pod-product-compliance
Lightning Source LLC
Chambersburg PA
CBHW080811120626
46556CB00009B/3285